MW01100211

Children's Storytime

"The little bear gave a sigh.
There was nothing to fear."

By the Light of the Moon, p.165

Children's Storytime

by
Nicola Baxter

ARMADILLO

First published in 2001 by Armadillo Books
An imprint of Bookmart Limited
Desford Road, Enderby
Leicester LE9 5AD, England

© 2001 Bookmart Limited

All rights reserved. No part of this publication may be reproduced,
stored in a retrieval system or transmitted by any means,
electronic, mechanical, photocopying or otherwise,
without the prior permission of the publisher.

Stories in this book were previously published in
My Book of Princess Stories, The Teddy Bear Collection,
The Bunny Tales Collection, The Puppy Tales Collection,
My Treasury of Stories and Rhymes, 5 Minute Bedtime Tales,
5 Minute Farmyard Tales, 5 Minute Kitten Tales,
5 Minute Teddy Bear Tales

ISBN 1-84322-025-3

Printed in Singapore

Contents

The Real Teddy Bear

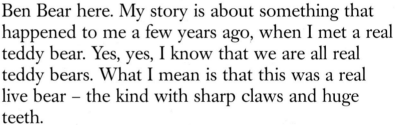

Ben Bear here. My story is about something that happened to me a few years ago, when I met a real teddy bear. Yes, yes, I know that we are all real teddy bears. What I mean is that this was a real live bear – the kind with sharp claws and huge teeth.

Here is what happened. My owner at the time was a little boy who was very fond of food. Wherever we went, he always made sure that he had a bag of goodies with him. "Just in case", he said, "we get caught in an avalanche, or stranded in the desert, or trapped by a flood." Not one of those things was at all likely to happen, but Joseph (that was his name) felt happier if he had some provisions with him.

You can imagine that this was particularly true when he went camping with his friends. All the boys brought food to cook on the campfire, but Joseph brought extra supplies, just in case.

6

One year, we went deep into the woods. The boys put up their tents and went off to explore. Joseph left me in his tent. Now that I am an older and wiser bear, I realize that he did not want his friends to see me, in case they thought he was a baby. But Joseph looked at me very seriously and said, "Now Ben, your job is to stay here and guard the food!" And I was a young bear who took his job seriously in those days.

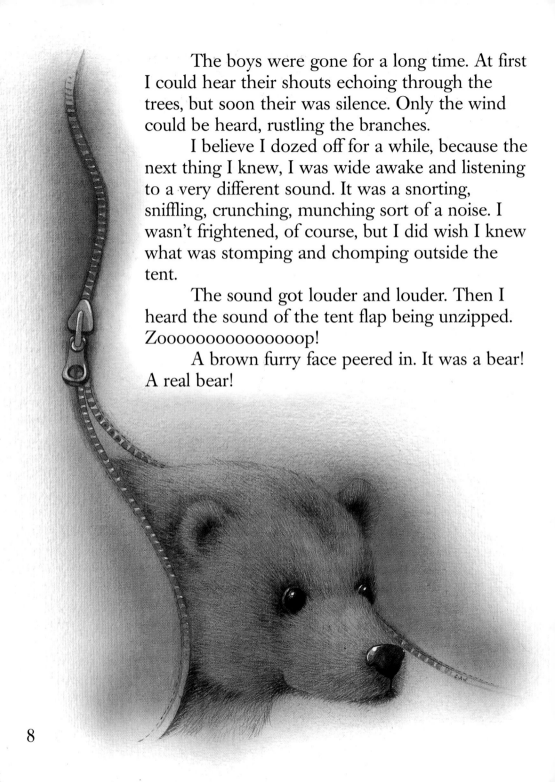

The boys were gone for a long time. At first I could hear their shouts echoing through the trees, but soon their was silence. Only the wind could be heard, rustling the branches.

I believe I dozed off for a while, because the next thing I knew, I was wide awake and listening to a very different sound. It was a snorting, sniffling, crunching, munching sort of a noise. I wasn't frightened, of course, but I did wish I knew what was stomping and chomping outside the tent.

The sound got louder and louder. Then I heard the sound of the tent flap being unzipped. Zoooooooooooooooop!

A brown furry face peered in. It was a bear! A real bear!

For a long, long moment, I looked at the bear. And the bear looked at me. Then, all of a sudden, he opened his mouth and said, "Hello! Anything to eat in here?"

Well, you could have knocked me down with a feather. He was speaking bear language of course, but I found it was not very different from the way we teddy bears speak, so I could understand him fairly well. He seemed friendly, and I was just thinking how nice it would be to get to know him, when I remembered what Joseph had said to me.

"No" I said firmly. "No food in here at all."

But the bear was already sniffing the air and looking suspiciously at the large bag beside me.

"Really?" he said. "That's very strange. I'm pretty sure I can smell sausages and beans and chocolate cake."

I thought quickly. "That's very clever of you." I said. "There *were* sausages and beans and chocolate cake, but the boys have eaten them all."

"Any leftovers?" asked the bear. "Any crumbs at all?"

"None at all," I replied, shaking my head sadly.

"More supplies coming?" asked the bear eagerly. "Tomorrow, perhaps?"

"I don't think so," I answered. "We're going home in the morning."

The bear nodded his head. "Ho hum," he said. "It's my birthday, you know. I just thought I might find a birthday treat around here somewhere. Well, nice to meet you." And as he ambled away into the forest, I was quite sure I could hear his furry tummy rumbling.

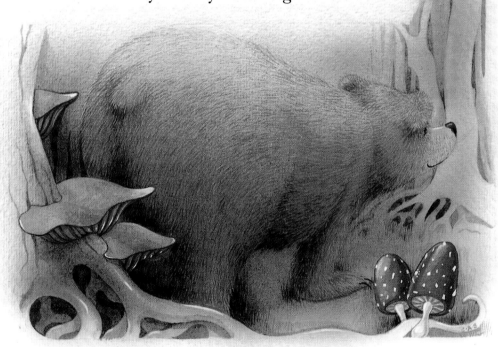

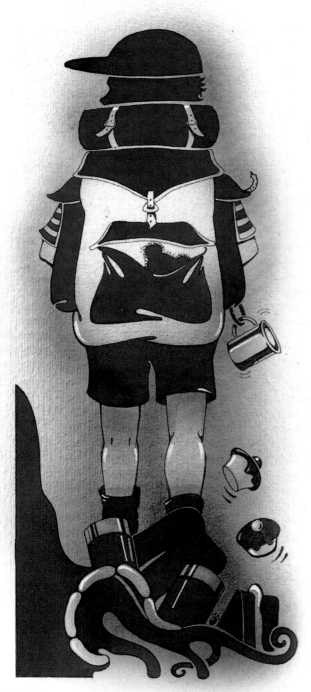

A little while later, the boys came back and made their supper. I kept a wary eye on the shadows between the trees, expecting to see some large furry ears or a sniffly snout. But there was no bear at all.

Next morning, as planned, we packed up our things and set off for home.

"Now, have we got everything?" asked Joseph. "Let's go!"

By this stage, of course, I was well hidden in Joseph's backpack, so that the other boys would not see me. Otherwise I might have mentioned to him that the special emergency supplies bag had fallen behind the stump of a tree, helped along just a bit by a nudge from my elbow.

Joseph was a little upset when he found that his goodies were gone. But it was far too late to go back into the dark forest to find them, and after all, there were plenty more at home.

As I sat on Joseph's pillow that night, I looked up at the big yellow moon peeking in at the window and imagined the friendly bear, sitting down in the moonlight to enjoy a special snack.

"Happy birthday, bear," I whispered. "Happy birthday!"

Little Pig Gets Lost

Although there were lots of piglets on Windytop Farm, one in particular caught Farmer Barnes' eye. Like his great uncle, Biggy Pig, he had all the signs of being a champion, and Farmer Barnes did like to win ribbons at the County Show. He called the piglet Little Pig.

Farmer Barnes wanted Little Pig to grow big, like you-know-who, but Little Pig surprised everyone by wanting to do sports!

Then, one day, Little Pig went missing. At first everyone thought he had gone for a longer run than usual, but when he didn't come back by lunchtime, and his feed trough was still full, all the animals began to get worried.

"He is only a little pig," said Duchess the cow. "He's not old enough to look after himself in the big, wide world."

"We need to search the farm," said Biggy. "The sheep can look in the meadows. I'll check the barns. The hens and ducks can look along the hedges and bushes. And you, Duchess, can wait here in case Little Pig comes home. I do hope he hasn't come to any harm."

But an hour later, the animals returned to the yard without Little Pig. They were now very worried indeed. They sat together, trying to think of a new plan. It was just then that Biggy's sharp ears heard a little squealing sound.

Hardly able to believe their eyes, the animals looked up, and up, and up . . . right to the top of the tree. A little pink face looked down at them. "I was climbing," said Little Pig, "but I got stuck!"

Busy Hen and Dymphna soon fluttered about and guided Little Pig down. He was very grateful.

You know, after that Little Pig wasn't quite so keen to test his sporting abilities.

"If you keep snuffling in your feed trough like that," said Busy Hen, "you'll soon be even bigger than Biggy Pig!" And he was.

15

The Big Bad Bunny

One morning, the little bunnies were being unusually annoying. When they bounced on Great-Uncle Otto's chair and broke the springs, that very wise old rabbit sighed and decided enough was was well and truly enough.

"You young bunnies should be careful," he warned, waving his willow walking stick. "If you're not careful, you'll find yourselves in a very sticky situation, just like the Big Bad Bunny."

"Oh, tell us, tell us!" called Pickles and Penny and all the other little bunnies.

"Very well," said Great-Uncle Otto, "but first you must find a cushion to put in my poor old chair and then you must sit absolutely still."

The little rabbits hurried to get ready. They loved the old rabbit's stories.

"The big bad bunny," Great-Uncle Otto began, "was once just an ordinary naughty little bunny – like you!"

17

The little bunnies wriggled in their seats, and Great-Uncle Otto went on.

"As this particular naughty little bunny got older," he said, "he also got bigger and badder, until he was a very big, very bad bunny indeed."

"What did he do?" squealed Pickles.

"He tied his sister's shoelaces together, so she fell over. He ate his brother's birthday cake *before* that poor little bunny's birthday. He shut his mother in the pantry while he made mud pies on the living room carpet. He put jelly in his father's slippers. He gathered a bunch of flowers for his auntie . . . from her own garden. He filled the bathtub with frogs and put worms in the kitchen sink. Need I say more?"

"Oooh!" said the little bunnies. "He *was* bad, wasn't he?"

"He was," said Great-Uncle Otto gravely, "but, as I said, he found himself in a sticky situation. Oh yes, a very sticky situation indeed."

"What happened?" squeaked Penny.

"Honey," replied her great-uncle briefly.

"Honey?"

"Yes, honey. One day, his mother left a big jar of honey on the table when she went shopping. Of course, the big bad bunny wanted to taste it. He dipped in one paw. Then that greedy bunny dipped in two paws. But, you know, that honey was very thick and gloopy. He found that his paws were completely stuck!

19

And when he bent his head to try and pull out his paws, his ears got stuck to the sticky jar as well! Of course, he struggled, and when his mother came home, she found him with the jar on his head and one ear and two paws stuck inside it, while gloopy, golden honey trickled slowly down his face. He was not a happy bunny."

"And was he good after that?" asked Pickles.

"He was," said Great-Uncle Otto firmly. "He became a fine, upstanding bunny, kind, er . . . wise, and respected by all. Now run along and play and let me read my book."

"What was the big bad bunny's name?" asked Penny, as the little bunnies ran out of the door.

"Hrrmph!" grunted her great-uncle. "Well, he happened to be called . . . ahem . . . Otto!"

21

The Most Beautiful Bear

"I am the most beautiful teddy bear in the world," thought Mopsybell. She could just see her reflection in the shop window. Her golden brown fur was fluffy. Her eyes were bright and shiny. She was sure that the next little girl to come into the shop would choose her.

Just then a little girl *did* come into the shop with her grandmother.

"Now Juliette," said Grandma. "You may choose which ever teddy bear you like best as a special present. Every little girl should have a teddy bear of her own."

The little girl scowled. "I don't really like bears," she said. "They're for babies. I'd much rather have a robot."

"Don't be silly, dear," said
Grandma. "You can't cuddle a robot.
Now, which bear would you like?"

Mopsybell wriggled on her shelf.
Just as she expected, she was going to
be chosen. But the little girl groaned.

"That's the most stupid-looking bear
I've ever seen," she said. Mopsybell was
so shocked, she nearly fell off her shelf.
What a horrible child!

But Grandma was determined. "If you
don't like that bear, dear choose another one,"
she said.

Juliette had wandered further into the shop.
"Pink?" she yelled. "I might be sick. Couldn't I
have this Dracula outfit? That reminds me of . . ."

"Juliette!" said Grandma quickly, "I've made
up my mind. I know you'll love this bear when
you get her home and she'll always remind you
of me. Now put those spiders down and let's
go home."

"I am still the most beautiful bear in the world," thought Mopysbell. "Juliette will know that as soon as she has a good look at me."

And sure enough, when Grandma had taken Juliette home and hurried off to catch her train, the little girl took a long hard look at her bear. "I can think of some uses for you after all," she said in a rather odd tone.

Mopsybell was just the right size for Juliette's parachute experiments. Tied to a pillow case, she was dropped out of every upstairs window in the house.

Then Juliette decided to start growing things instead. She spent ages digging in the garden and watching worms. Then she sprinkled some seeds on the ground and tied Mopsybell to a post nearby.

"I found your bear in the garden, Juliette," said her mother that night. "You must have forgotten her."

"No." explained Juliette. "She's a scarecrow, keeping the birds away from my seeds."

"A scarecrow! I shall die of shame," thought Mopsybell.

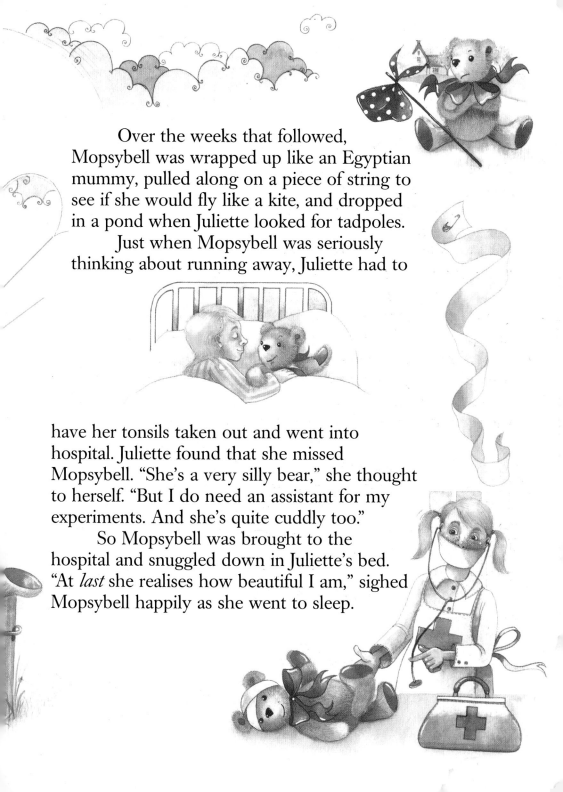

Over the weeks that followed, Mopsybell was wrapped up like an Egyptian mummy, pulled along on a piece of string to see if she would fly like a kite, and dropped in a pond when Juliette looked for tadpoles.

Just when Mopsybell was seriously thinking about running away, Juliette had to have her tonsils taken out and went into hospital. Juliette found that she missed Mopsybell. "She's a very silly bear," she thought to herself. "But I do need an assistant for my experiments. And she's quite cuddly too."

So Mopsybell was brought to the hospital and snuggled down in Juliette's bed. "At *last* she realises how beautiful I am," sighed Mopsybell happily as she went to sleep.

The Trouble With Denby Dog

Farmer Barnes took good care of all his animals, but Denby Dog was special. He had worked with the farmer for more years than either of them could remember.

But Denby Dog was getting old. He found it harder to run after the tractors Farmer Barnes drove out of the yard. His legs felt stiff as he trotted up the lane. Even his bark was not as loud as it used to be.

As winter approached, Farmer Barnes became more and more worried about Denby.

"Old Fellow," he said, "the wind is bitter this morning. Why not stay beside the fire or in your kennel in the yard? I can manage without you today."

But the old dog gave Farmer Barnes such a mournful look that he couldn't bear to leave him behind. Later, Denby Dog explained to his friend Biggy Pig how he felt. "I've been with Farmer Barnes for years, pup and dog," he said.

"What if something happened to him away in the fields and I wasn't there to run for help? I'd never forgive myself. No, while there's life in these old bones, I must do my job."

Strangely enough, it was also to Biggy Pig that Farmer Barnes explained his worries that evening. He leaned over the sty wall and scratched Biggy's back.

"It's like this," he said. "Old Denby simply isn't up to the job any more. I've bought a new pup. He'll be arriving tomorrow, but I hate the idea of hurting the old boy's feelings."

Biggy Pig snorted in a comforting sort of way. He felt sure everything would be fine. And it was.

When the new puppy arrived, Denby Dog got straight down to business. "It's high time I retired, young pup," he said. "And now that there'll be someone to follow in my paw prints, I can do it at last. But first, there's a lot I've got to teach you. Follow me now, and leave those chickens alone!"

These days, Denby Dog has a leisurely life, chatting with his friends and lying in the sun. After all, he deserves it.

The Prettiest Princess

Once upon a time, in a land far away, there lived a Princess who was very pretty. And she knew it. She grew up hearing the admiring gasps of everyone who saw her.

"How pretty she is!" "She is the loveliest little girl I've ever seen!" "Her beauty is dazzling!" Those are the kinds of things Princess Aisla heard on every side. The people who said them weren't being flattering or trying to compliment her parents. It was simply true. She was the prettiest Princess in the world.

Now, you might think a Princess who heard nothing but compliments all day long would be conceited and disagreeable. At the very least, you would expect her to spend hours in front of the mirror every day, brushing her beautiful hair and curling her eyelashes.

But you would be wrong. Princess Aisla was the sweetest, kindest, friendliest girl you could ever meet. And clever, too. Much cleverer than all her sisters.

"It isn't fair!" said Bethany one day.

"I couldn't agree more," said Camilla, pulling at her perfectly nice (but not dazzling) golden hair.

"But there's nothing we can do about it," said Dahlia, frowning. "I've brushed my hair until my arm aches, and it still doesn't shine like Aisla's."

"Maybe we're going about this the wrong way," said Camilla thoughtfully. "It's not that we need to be prettier. It's that Aisla needs to be *uglier*."

And that is why, late one night, three cloaked figures left the castle and crept down the path to the ancient Forest of Gloom.

There are no prizes for guessing how the forest got it's name. Even in daylight it was a dark and scary place. At night, it was worse. The sisters trembled at every step.

Deep in the forest lived a wizard with a dreadful reputation. All the children were warned *never* to go near him. Those that did, they were told, would be turned into toads and have to live in the Forest of Gloom forever.

The Princesses came at last to the wizard's lair. Much to their surprise, he turned out to be a friendly looking old man with twinkling eyes and a half-munched cherry muffin in his hand. It wasn't what they had been expecting at all.

"There's no need to tell me why you've come, or what you're thinking," said the wizard to his visitors. "I can solve your problems in two seconds. Do you know why you were surprised by my appearance?"

"It's . . . well . . . we . . ." stuttered Bethany. But the wizard interrupted her.

"It's because you think someone who looks jolly and friendly must be good and kind," he said. "While someone who looks ugly and frightening must be spiteful and nasty. Well, it simply isn't true, you know. I, for example, am quite a nasty character. You're lucky to have met me *after* I've had my lunch!"

The Princesses felt uneasy. They also didn't understand *what* he was talking about.

"You mean our sister isn't good and kind?" asked Camilla, puzzled.

"On the contrary," said the wizard. "She is very good and kind, but she isn't *happy.*"

"Not happy?" Such a thing had never occured to the sisters. Surely someone who was admired so much, who was good at everything she did, who never had to worry about spots or geography homework or being unpopular couldn't be unhappy? Could she?

The sisters hurried home through the Forest of Gloom, their thoughts whirling.

Next morning, they looked at their sister with new eyes. She was pretty. She was clever. She loved everyone. But it didn't mean a thing. Now they could see that she was sad inside. Suddenly, Bethany, Camilla and Dahlia stopped hating their sister and started to want to help her.

These days, if you visit the castle on the hill beyond the Forest of Gloom, you will find four beautiful, happy sisters, and you would find it hard to tell which was the prettiest. A Princess whose eyes are glowing and heart is laughing is always lovely – and loved.

A Very Wobbly Chimney

Sir Woofington Paws lived in a large house a mile or so from the town of Houndsville. Unfortunately, although his family had once been very wealthy, Sir Woofington was now in reduced circumstances. This was mostly his father's fault. Old Sir Patchmont Paws had been a great collector. Unfortunately, he hadn't the vaguest idea what to collect. His famous art collection had turned out to be the work of a small team of professional forgers who could turn their paws to any style or period. Yes, even the famous picture of the Dogs Palace in Venice by Kenneletto was proved to be the work of Towser "The Paintbrush" Terrier, a dog well known to the Pooch Police.

It was the same with Sir Patchmont's collection of fine silver. He had bought it in good faith from a shifty-looking dog who knocked at the door one day. Only a week later, it was discovered that every single piece had been stolen from Duchess Dulay. Of course, it had to be returned.

I need hardly mention what happened to Sir Patchmont's ice sculpture collection one hot June, or the most unfortunate scene when he discovered two of his nephews munching their way through his very expensive bone collection. It is enough to say that by the time he had finished, Sir Patchmont Paws had lost almost all the family money, leaving his son, Sir Woofington, to try to keep up appearances on a shoestring.

It had once been widely believed in Houndsville that Sir Woofington would marry the widowed Duchess Dulay, but he could not bring himself to propose to her when he had no way of supporting her. So Sir Woofington lived alone in his crumbling home, looking sadly at the spaces on the walls where his father's fake pictures had once hung.

Now Paws Place was literally falling down around Sir Woofington's ears. He couldn't afford to hire professionals to fix his roof or check his plumbing, so he did it himself. Sadly, Sir Woofington's home-improvement skills were dreadfully bad. He frequently made matters worse instead of better.

One morning, Sir Woofington was chopping wood outside the back door when he happened to look up. As he did so, a tiny bird landed on one of the tallest chimneys of the house, and . . . there could be no doubt about it . . . it quite distinctly wobbled. The chimney wobbled. The bird wobbled. And Sir Woofington, watching this with a sinking heart, felt his knees wobble too.

I'm afraid that Sir Woofington inherited his brains from his father. Before you could say, "Don't even think about it, Sir W!" he hurried off to find the very longest ladder in his workshop.

Without waiting for someone to come and help him, Sir Woofington started to climb. Up, up, up he went. And wobble, wobble, wobble went the ladder. Every step brought him nearer to disaster – and every step was wobblier than the one before. But the silly dog kept climbing.

Just as Sir Woofington reached the base of the wobbly chimney, a car drove into his driveway. The climbing dog looked down. As he turned his head, the ladder slipped away, leaving him clinging to the chimney.

Sir Woofington Paws thought his last moments had come. In a faint voice, he called for help. Now that he was close to it, he could see that the chimney was likely to fall down in the slightest breeze. It certainly was not strong enough to support a full-grown dog.

Far below, a dog that Sir Woofington had never seen before looked up in horror at the dangling figure. He spotted a little window not far from Sir Woofington's left paw and, without waiting to knock or introduce himself, he rushed into the house and up the stairs. Just as Sir Woofington felt that he would have to let go, the strange dog grabbed him firmly with a large paw.

Half an hour later, Sir Woofington and his guests were drinking tea in the shabby dining room. (Sir Woofington couldn't afford real houndstooth tea, but his garden was full of nettles.) It was only then, after offering heartfelt thanks, that Sir Woofington asked his visitor why he had come.

To his host's surprise, the large dog flushed pink. "I have come," he said "to put right a bad thing I did many years ago. When I was a young dog," he went on, "I turned to crime. One day I robbed the home of a rich dog in Houndsville and sold her silver to your father."

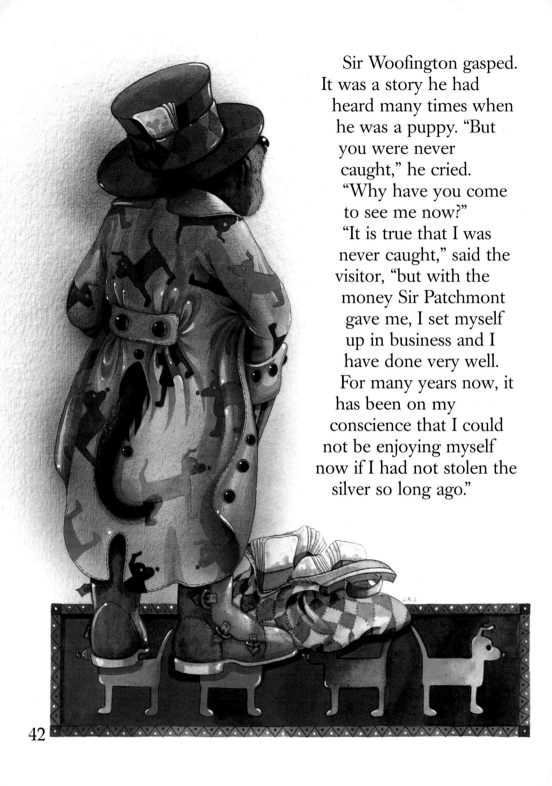

Sir Woofington gasped. It was a story he had heard many times when he was a puppy. "But you were never caught," he cried. "Why have you come to see me now?"

"It is true that I was never caught," said the visitor, "but with the money Sir Patchmont gave me, I set myself up in business and I have done very well. For many years now, it has been on my conscience that I could not be enjoying myself now if I had not stolen the silver so long ago."

"My dear sir," cried Sir Woofington, "this morning you saved my life. What is past is past. I am only too happy to forget the whole thing."

But the stranger shook his head. "You deserve to have half my wealth," he said. "There is plenty for both of us."

So that is how Sir Woofington's fortunes were restored. He is once more seen in the best circles in Houndsville. Paws Place has been repaired by skilled dogs and filled with fine furniture and some (absolutely genuine) pictures. And it is said that Duchess Dulay has been seen dining there recently on more than one occasion!

There's a Bear in the Bathroom!

"Hey!" yelled Charlie one evening. "There's a bear in the bathroom!"

"Charlie!" shouted his mother. "I've got enough to do looking after the baby, without listening to silly stories from you."

The bear smiled at Charlie and turned on the water for him. Then it politely covered up it's eyes while he got undressed and into the bath.

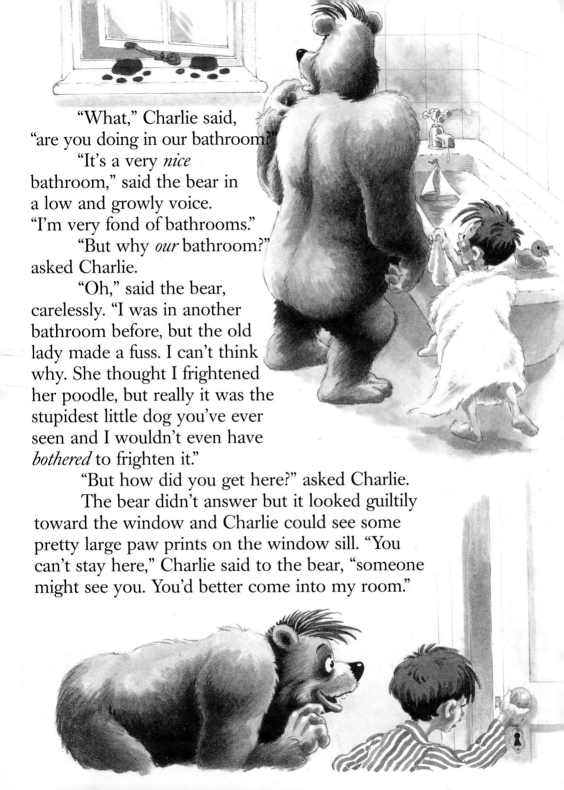

"What," Charlie said, "are you doing in our bathroom?"

"It's a very *nice* bathroom," said the bear in a low and growly voice. "I'm very fond of bathrooms."

"But why *our* bathroom?" asked Charlie.

"Oh," said the bear, carelessly. "I was in another bathroom before, but the old lady made a fuss. I can't think why. She thought I frightened her poodle, but really it was the stupidest little dog you've ever seen and I wouldn't even have *bothered* to frighten it."

"But how did you get here?" asked Charlie.

The bear didn't answer but it looked guiltily toward the window and Charlie could see some pretty large paw prints on the window sill. "You can't stay here," Charlie said to the bear, "someone might see you. You'd better come into my room."

Charlie took the bear into his room and gave him a half eaten bag of soggy potato chips. The bear ate them happily and Charlie began to see useful possibilities for the horrible carrots that his mother insisted on serving.

"Were you planning on staying long?" he asked the bear as politely as he could.

"Only as long as it is convenient," replied the bear. "I thought you might like some company at the moment."

Charlie sighed. It was true. Ever since his little baby brother had been born a few weeks before, it seemed no one had any time for *him*.

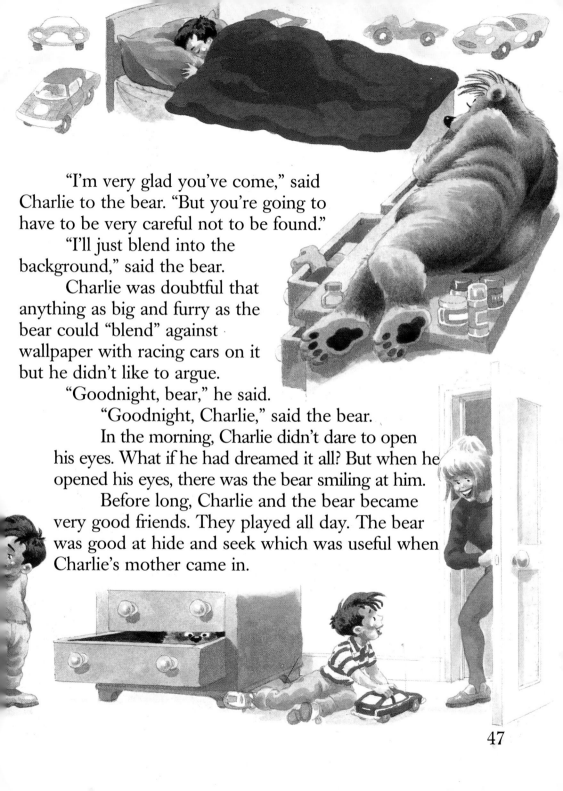

"I'm very glad you've come," said Charlie to the bear. "But you're going to have to be very careful not to be found."

"I'll just blend into the background," said the bear.

Charlie was doubtful that anything as big and furry as the bear could "blend" against wallpaper with racing cars on it but he didn't like to argue.

"Goodnight, bear," he said.

"Goodnight, Charlie," said the bear.

In the morning, Charlie didn't dare to open his eyes. What if he had dreamed it all? But when he opened his eyes, there was the bear smiling at him.

Before long, Charlie and the bear became very good friends. They played all day. The bear was good at hide and seek which was useful when Charlie's mother came in.

"It's not good for you to be all by yourself, Charlie," said his mother. "Why don't you come and play with your brother? He's crawling now."

The bear turned out to be the perfect kind of friend. When Charlie was sad, it gave him a big furry hug. When he was happy, it made funny bear-faces that made Charlie laugh so much his tummy ached.

One day, Charlie went downstairs to find some apples for the bear and got quite a suprise. In the living room, his little brother was standing up holding onto the arm of a chair. He looked up, smiling all over his little face, and said, "Charlie!"

Charlie looked down. The little kid wasn't so bad at all and he liked the idea of being a big brother. Charlie bent down and looked carefully at the little boy, who had let go of the chair with his chubby hands and was tottering toward Charlie. Then he fell forward and held onto Charlie's knees.

Charlie sat on the floor and helped his little brother to stand up. He was even warmer and cuddlier than the bear and he smiled up at Charlie with a friendly little face. Charlie forgot all about food for the bear and played until suppertime.

When Charlie went to bed, he thought for a minute about telling the bear all about his little brother. But he wasn't very suprised to find that the bear was nowhere to be seen and there were big black paw prints on the window sill.

The Cluckety Duck

Farmer Barnes' duckpond was never a very peaceful place. Those ducks were always making a noise.

One day, Farmer Barnes brought a new duck to the pond.

"Be nice to her, you daffy ducks," he said. "She's not used to your quacky, splashy ways."

For several days, the little duck paddled shyly around the pond and didn't say a word. At last Dymphna, who was curious about the newcomer, waddled up and asked her how she was finding her new home. The duck looked up and opened her beak. She said her first word on Windytop Farm. It was … "Cluck!"

Dymphna was so surprised that she sat down plop! on her newly curled tail feathers. Whoever heard of a clucking duck? And the trouble was that none of the ducks could understand a word she clucked.

Dymphna knew that she would have to talk to Busy Hen. It was well known that Busy Hen knew several foreign languages, but Dymphna and Busy Hen were not the best of friends.

Later that day, the farmyard animals saw Busy Hen deep in conversation with the newcomer, fluffing her feathers and chatting as if they had been friends for years.

"It's quite simple," she told Dymphna that evening. "This little duck is an orphan. She was brought up by an old lady's French hen. So of course, she has never learned to speak duck language. We will have to teach her."

The new duck, whose name was Daphne, was a very quick pupil. How proud of her Dymphna and Busy Hen were when she first dived into the pond with a loud, "QUACK!"

I'm afraid the duckpond is noisier than ever these days!

51

The Buzzing Bear

Now, bear language is very interesting to study. I am Professor Septimus Bear and I have spent a good deal of my life looking into the different forms of bear talk, but I must confess that one case made me appear to be a rather silly old bear.

I was living at that time in a large house in Canada. In the summer, children would come to visit my own family, and, of course, they would bring their bears with them. That was how I met the buzzing bear.

This bear came to the house on a fine, sunny day. He was a large, fluffy bear with golden yellow fur. Of course, I tried to make him welcome.

"Good morning," I said. "My name is Septimus. Will you tell me yours?"

"Buzz!" said the bear.

"Er . . . Buzz? Well it's very nice to meet you, Mr Buzz. Have you had a long journey?"

"Buzz!" said the bear.

"I'm sorry? Did you say that you have come from far away?"

"Buzz! Buzz! Buzz!" said the strange bear.

Well, I must admit, I was puzzled. I went to my reference books to find out if there was a distant country where bears only buzzed. I read and read until darkness fell.

53

But all my research was in vain. I read about the hooting bears of Borneo and the singing bears of Thailand. I found an article about an African bear language that has all kinds of sounds in it and it is impossible for other bears to pronounce. But I could find nothing at all about buzzing bears.

I was disappointed at first. Then I realised the great opportunity that had been presented to me. I could be the very first bear to study this extraordinary language. I saw myself giving lectures to other clever bears around the world. I imagined signing copies of my famous book on the subject. A rosy future was surely before me.

At once, I picked up a new notebook and pencil and set off to find the bear.

The buzzing bear was sitting rather sadly in a chair. I sat down beside him and began to take notes as I asked him questions.

"Are you a bear?" I asked.

"Buzz!" he said.

Aha, I thought, one buzz means yes.

"Are you an elephant?" I asked.

"Buzz! Buzz!" said the bear.

I decided that two buzzes must mean no.

"Are you a giraffe?" I enquired.

"Buzz!"

My friends, I admit I was very confused. Then I realised that the bear might not be able to understand me at all! But how was I supposed to learn buzz language in order to speak to him? I did not know how to say the simplest thing.

It was a beautiful day, so I took the bear by the arm and led him gently out into the garden. By the house was an enormous cedar tree. I led the bear up to it and patted its trunk firmly.

"Tree," I said. "Tree."

"Buzz!" said the bear.

I walked over to a shady seat.

"Chair," I repeated, pointing. "Chair. Chair"

You can probably guess what the bear said.

After half an hour, I was at my wit's end. We had made no progress at all and I was afraid that my reputation as a scholar was at stake. Would anyone ever take my work seriously again, I wondered?

At last, tired and depressed, I invited the bear to sit down by a beautiful flower border.

We had only been sitting for a minute when, "Buzz! BUZZ! BUZZZ!"

The loudest buzzing I had ever heard filled my ears. And out of the strange bear's ears flew first one and then another big, yellow, buzzing bee!

"What a relief!" said the bear. "I haven't been able to hear a thing with those bees buzzing in there!"

Well, we both rolled on the grass laughing, and I have tried hard not to be such a pompous old bear ever since!

The Carrot Collection

Tempers in the Big Burrow became a little frayed when Penny and Pickles started collecting things. They had a friend who collected postcards, but they thought that was pretty boring. Both of them wanted to collect something much more exciting than that.

"I'm going to collect leaves," said Penny. "They're very interesting, and there are all sorts of different kinds."

"I'm going to collect caterpillars," said Pickles. "There are lots of different kinds of them too, and they can crawl, you know, which is much, much more exciting."

"Hmmm," Penny was not so sure. Dimly in the back of her mind, she felt that there might be a problem if caterpillars began crawling around in the Big Burrow. But it was impossible to change Pickles' mind once he had decided on something. Before long, every corner of his bedroom was filled with little jars and pots, covered with paper lids in which Pickles had carefully punched little holes.

"I hope you're giving those caterpillars plenty to eat," said Father Rabbit, looking suspiciously at the jars. "Caterpillars who are hungry might have a tendency to roam."

But Pickles took very good care of his caterpillars. In fact, he was so interested in them that he didn't even notice what Penny was doing.

Unfortunately, the day came when it was raining so hard that Pickles could not go outside to find leaves for his creepy-crawly friends. He was beginning to get desperate when he noticed a pile of leaves in the corner of the hallway outside the dining room.

"Those will be fine," said Pickles.

It was not until that evening, when Pickles' caterpillars had done quite a bit of chomping and chewing, that Penny was heard to shout from the middle of the burrow, "Who's moved my leaf collection?" Pickles hid under the bed for a very long time.

Next morning, it seemed that Pickles, too, had troubles. Each one of his caterpillars had turned into a hard, shiny thing that didn't move at all. Pickles left all his jars open in disgust.

"I can't understand you young rabbits," said Father Rabbit, when he saw the two little ones sitting sadly on the stairs. "In my day we used to collect something useful . . . like carrots! Why, I remember having the biggest and best carrot collection in all of Warren Wood. Let me tell you about it. Storage was the biggest problem, but I had a clever idea . . ."

Now this was not the first time that the little rabbits had heard about Father Rabbit's famous carrot collection, and they were very sorry indeed that they'd given him the opportunity to tell them about it all over again. He even had photographs of the collection, which he eagerly dug out of a drawer. Between you and me, there are few things more boring than photographs of carrots, especially photographs of hundreds of carrots in rows. The carrot stories went on for days.

Finally, the little rabbits could stand it no longer. "Er . . . I must go and clear up my bedroom," said Pickles, which was such an unusual thing for him to say that Penny fell off her chair in surprise. But when she had picked herself up, she half remembered that she had promised to help Pickles, and she hurried off to join him.

And when the rabbits opened the door of
Pickles' bedroom, they had the most wonderful surprise.
Every one of the hard, shiny things had hatched . . .

. . . into a beautiful, fluttering butterfly.

63

Oh No, Not Again!

There was once a little elf called Juniper Jingle who lived in a tree trunk with his mother and his granny.

But Juniper's mother and granny found him very hard to live with. You see, Juniper had wonderful dreams, but they always had the same result. Juniper tossed and turned so much in his sleep that he fell out of bed. And when Juniper fell with a thud, the whole tree shook and everyone woke up, except Juniper Jingle, who slept on as if nothing had happened … on the floor.

Mrs. Jingle had tried everything to keep Juniper in his bed. Finally, she decided she must go to see the Fidget Fairy for a magic spell.

The Fidget Fairy knew at once what to do.

"Juniper is a most extraordinary elf. An imagination like that should be encouraged. I will give you a spell to make him an imaginary bed, and everything will be well."

Mrs. Jingle was not convinced, but when she got home she said the spell exactly as she had been taught it. At once, Juniper's old bed disappeared … and nothing came in its place. Mrs. Jingle was just about to go back to the fairy to complain when Juniper walked in.

"Wow!" he said. "Wow and double wow! That's a wonderful bed!" And he climbed up into mid-air and lay there, as comfortable as could be.

Juniper still has wonderful dreams, but no matter how much he tosses and turns, he never hits the floor. And everyone else is happy, too.

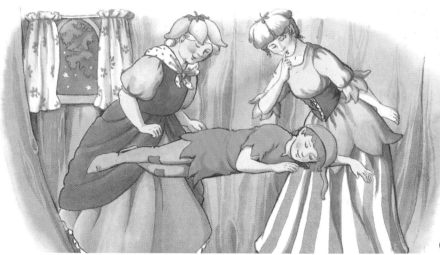

The Princess and the Unicorn

Once upon a time, there was a very beautiful Princess. She lived in a fairytale castle, surrounded by the prettiest gardens you have ever seen. She had everything that a Princess could desire, and she was a clever girl too. But – and this is very strange – she didn't believe in magic!

Now in stories, Princesses are always coming across good fairies and bad fairies, witches and wizards, elves and pixies. They meet frogs who can talk and little men who can spin straw into gold. In fact, there seems to be magic all over the place.

But this Princess, whose name was Cariana, had never seen a fairy or an elf. No one had put a spell on her to send her to sleep for a hundred years. She had not been imprisoned by a witch. Her cat and dog meowed and barked but did not say a word in human language. So perhaps it was not really at all surprising that she did not believe in magic at all.

"I'll believe in it," she said with a laugh, "when I can see it with my own eyes, and not until then."

One day, Princess Cariana went for a walk in the woods. It was a beautiful, sunny day. The birds sang in the trees and her little dog, Plum, enjoyed sniffing here and there among the roots of the trees and burying his nose in the woodland flowers.

"Who needs magic when the real world is so beautiful?" The Princess smiled.

Perhaps it was because she was feeling so happy that the young Princess walked further than she ever had done before. It seemed that the further she went, the more lovely the trees and flowers became. Surely the sunlight had never sparkled so brightly? Every leaf and flower seemed to have it's own golden light, and a sweet perfume filled the air. The Princess could not bear to turn back from such beauty, so she walked on and on. At last she sank down on a flowery bank.

"I will just rest here for a moment," she told her little dog.

Plum snuffled happily under some bushes for a while. When he looked up at the Princess again, she was sleeping peacefully among the flowers. Plum settled down at her feet, but he did not go to sleep. He knew it was his duty to guard his mistress.

The Princess must have been very tired indeed, for she slept for a long time. When she finally opened her eyes, the sun was just setting, and a soft, warm darkness was falling over the woods.

"I must hurry home!" cried the Princess.

Scrambling to her feet, the Princess set off along the path, but it was hard now to see where she was going, although little glowing insects hovered among the trees. After she had taken only a few steps, the Princess caught her foot in a tree root and tumbled to the ground.

"Oh, Plum," she cried, "I have hurt my ankle. I don't think I can walk any further. What will happen to us?" With a sigh, she fainted clean away. (You must remember that she had led a very sheltered life and was not used to having to face difficulties and dangers.)

Plum stood guard over his mistress, looking nervously about him. Suddenly, the woods that had seemed so lovely before became full of strange rustling, breathing noises. There were little squeaks and scufflings that he had never noticed in the daylight. Plum knew that the woods might be full of dangerous animals. There could be snakes or wolves or even – and this was a really horrible thought – bears! Sure enough, a second or two later the little dog heard the sound of a really big animal crashing toward him – fast!

As the brave little dog prepared to defend his mistress with his life, a shimmering white shape appeared through the trees. It was a unicorn!

Gently, the beautiful white animal lowered his silver horn and lifted the Princess onto his back. Then he lowered his head again and looked at the little dog. Plum thought he had never seen such kind, wise eyes. He knew at once that everything would be fine and let himself be lifted up beside his mistress.

Plum never forgot the magical ride through the trees that followed. It was as if the unicorn's hooves hardly touched the ground.

Before long, the lighted castle appeared before them. The unicorn laid the Princess gently in the gardens and vanished into the night.

Now it was Plums turn. Barking as loudly as he could, he summoned help from the castle.

The Princess's ankle was soon better. Ever afterward, she was careful not to stray too far into the forest, but she had no memory of what had happened.

To this day, the Princess still doesn't believe in magic . . .
But Plum does!

Birthday Books

Grown-up people can be very bad at remembering things. So how is it they (usually) remember your birthday? That's the work of the birthday fairy, who whispers in their ears a week or so before each important day.

The fairies have a special book, where all the birthdays in the world are written down. They are all kept in the Lilac Library. A very old elf has been the librarian for years and years. He is helped by a team of lively little elves.

One day, there was a terrible commotion in the Lilac Library. A book had gone missing! It was the one for October 17th, Volume 96.

The elves searched all day. Then they lit little lamps and searched all night. But they could not find the missing book.

The fairy concerned was beside herself with anxiety. "Don't worry, my dear," cried the Chief Librarian. "Come back in half an hour and I'll have a list of names for you."

As soon as the fairy had gone, the old elf pressed a secret button under his desk. A whole shelf of books swung open, and the Librarian slipped inside to his secret room. There was a computer with a smile on its screen.

"Can I help you, Librarian?" it asked. In no time at all, a long list of all the birthdays for October 17th curled out of the machine.

The fairy was delighted with the list and promised not to tell about the back-up system. And the Librarian soon found he had been sitting on the missing volume all the time!

Wind Who Went Away

Once upon a time, there was a fierce and fearsome wind who blew all day long around the village of Belton.

The good people of Belton got together to decide what to do.

"We could build another wind-mill to use up the wind," suggested one man, but the miller objected that his business would be halved.

"We could stay indoors," suggested an old lady who didn't get out much anyway.

"We could pay the wind to go away," said the bank manager.

In the end, no one could agree about what to do, so the people went home to their houses, blown and buffeted all the way.

Now, the wily old wind had been listening. He decided he would teach the villagers a lesson.

There and then, he packed his bags and went off to the mountains.

The next day, everything was still. For a few hours, everyone was very happy. Then the complaints began. "I can't fly my kite!" cried the miller's son.

"My laundry won't get dry!" groaned the greengrocer.

"The sailing ship bringing my goods from China is stuck out in the bay," said a merchant.

I wish I could say that the people of Belton are more careful now about complaining, but they're not. The other day, I heard them moaning that the summer was too hot. I'm very much afraid the sun heard them too.

The Bear Who Was Bare

This is the story about a bare bear. A bare bear? I mean, of course, a bear wearing nothing at all - not even his fur! Let me tell you how it happened.

Once there was a bear called Edwin Dalrymple
Devereux Yeldon III. He said that his friends called
him Eddy, but as a matter of fact, this bear did not
have many friends at all. And that was because he
was simply not a very nice bear. Oh, he was very
handsome, with long, golden fur that shone in the
sunlight, but that was where the problem began.
Eddy thought that he was better than other bears,
with his long name and fancy fur.

"Pass me my fur brush," he would say. "The breeze has ruffled me terribly. You other bears need not worry, of course, with your short, rough, ordina fur."

When the bears played leap-bear or hide-and seek in the nursery, Eddy always refused to play.

"Those are very rough games," he complained "I might get my paws dirty. Games are too silly for superior bears like myself."

Well, after a while, all the other bears were sick of Edwin and his airs and graces. I'm afraid tha some young bears tried to think of ways of teachin Eddy a lesson. But as things turned out, they did not need to. Edwin Dalrymple Devereux Yeldon II brought about his own downfall.

One day, Eddy was boasting about all the famous bears he knew. One or two of the other bears wondered out loud if his tales were really true, which made Eddy furious. "You'll see," he said. "I'll write a letter to my friend Prince Bearovski. He's sure to write back at once, and then you'll see."

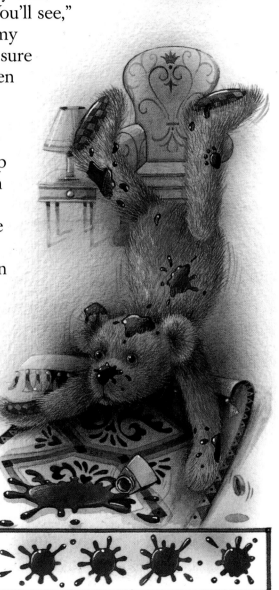

But as Eddy carried a huge bottle of ink across the room, his furry feet tripped up on the edge of the rug. Down fell teddy Eddy. Up flew the bottle of ink. *Splat!* The bottle hit the floor, and ink flew everywhere! There was ink on Eddy's nose and ink on his ears. His paws and knees had bright splashes too.

For a second, there was silence. Then Eddy let out a terrible roar. "You stupid bears!" he cried. "Just look at my fur! Who put that rug in the way?" And that was not really fair, for the rug had been there for years and years.

Teddy Eddy sulked for the rest of the day. But worse was to follow. Next morning, the little girl who lived there saw what had happened to her most beautiful bear. Without asking anyone else at all, she decided that Eddy needed a bath.

The other bears peeked around the bathroom door to watch the proceedings.

The bath was full of bubbles and only the tip of Eddy's nose could be seen. Giggling and chuckling, the bears went back into the nursery and waited for Eddy to reappear.

They waited all day and all that night. But Eddy did not return. Next day, there was still no sign of him.

"That little girl is not very sensible," said one bear. "She may have left him in the water. We really should go and see if he's all right, my friends."

But teddy Eddy was not in the bathtub. The bears were just about to go away again, when one little bear noticed that one of the cupboards was not quite closed.

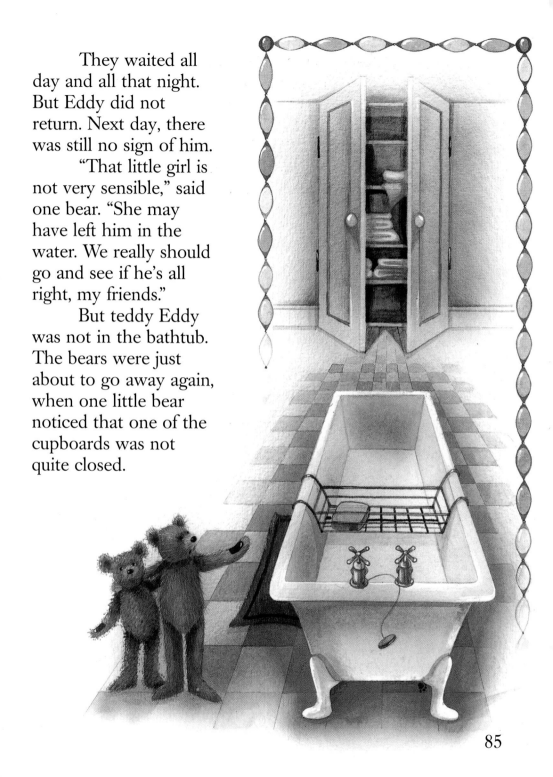

Inside was sat Edwin Dalrymple Devereux
Yeldon III, wrapped from ears to paws in a large
towel.

"Come on, Eddy," called the young bear
mischievously, "you must be dry now."

"No," said Eddy. "I . . . er . . . can't."

"But it must be very boring in this
cupboard," said another bear.

"No," said Eddy. "It's . . . er . . . very
pleasant. Please go away."

"Oh come on," two of the smallest bears
laughed. And they tugged playfully at the towel.
Eddy tried hard to hold onto it, but it was no use.
As the towel slipped away, every bear could see
that . . . Edwin Dalrymple Devereux Yeldon III was
bare! When the little girl washed away the ink,
Eddy's fur was washed away too.

Poor Eddy. He couldn't hide anymore. Slowly, he walked back to the nursery and sat down in the darkest corner. The old, proud Edwin Dalrymple Devereux Yeldon III was gone. A very different bear remained.

For a few days, the other bears smiled to themselves about what had happened. But after a while, they began to feel rather sorry for Eddy.

"I think we should help him," said one old bear. "Apart from anything else, he must be cold without his fur."

"That's true," another bear agreed. "Why don't we make him some clothes?"

Over the next few days, the bears had great fun. They used up all the old scraps of material that they could find and made some very grand clothes. There was a hat with a feather, a long cloak with tassels, striped trousers, and some black shiny boots.

When he saw them, Eddy was overwhelmed by the bears' kindness.

"Thank you, my friends," he said, as he put on the clothes. "I know that I have not been a very nice bear in the past, but I will do better now. In following all that is good and kind and bearlike, I will be absolutely fearless. Or perhaps I should say, in spite of my fine clothes, my dears, absolutely furless!"

The Magic Quilt

Once upon a time, there was a woman who loved to sew. She made beautiful dresses for her daughters and fine suits for her sons.

But the years passed. One by one, her children left home and scttled in faraway lands. From time to time, they sent letters home to their mother, but in all her busy life, she had never learned to read. She kept the letters in a chest, tied up with ribbons, until a friend from the nearby town could come to tell her what they said.

As the woman grew older, she could no longer work. At last, she became too weak to look after herself. Her friend invited her to stay. All she took with her was the chest from the foot of her bed.

"If only you could read," said her friend, "it would give you something to do all day."

Next morning, the woman suddenly knew what she must do. She asked her friend to open up her old chest and put it within her reach. Inside, as well as the letters from her children, there were all the scraps of fabric left over from her sewing over the years. Very carefully, she cut them into rectangles, like the pages of a book. Slowly, with stiff fingers, she sewed them together, until she had used all the pieces.

The beautiful quilt covered the old woman's bed from top to toe. As she smoothed her fingers over the fabric, in her mind she journeyed to far off places, thinking of the memories held by each piece of fabric.

"This is a book that I can read," she said, and she never felt unhappy again.

The Mighty Mouse

One morning at school, Mrs. Mumbles told the little kittens all about mice. Now kittens and cats are very interested in mice, as you can imagine, but these days, with good home cooking and lots of stores where cats can buy food, many younger kittens have never come face to face with a real live mouse.

In the playground after the lesson, Bella was pretending to know everything as usual.

"Ordinary mice are no problem," she said. "What you need to worry about are giant mice. They are twice as big as a grown-up cat and twice as fierce."

The little kittens were impressed by this. They tried to imagine what a giant mouse might look like, but since they had never seen even an ordinary mouse, that was difficult.

That evening, Rolypoly tossed and turned in his bed. Every time he closed his eyes, he seemed to see the staring eyes of a

monster that just might be a giant mouse. At last, unable to sleep, he crept out of bed and tiptoed toward the kitchen. There was a little lamp shining in the hallway.

"Aaaaaah!" he squeaked, his little heart thudding. There on the wall was a giant shadow. It had whiskers! It had a tail! It was a giant mouse, and it was right behind him!

With another squeal, Rolypoly ran into the living room.

"What on earth is the matter?" gasped Mamma cat.

But when he told Mamma what had happened, she laughed.

"Come with me, Rolypoly," she said, leading him into the hallway, where there were now two giant shadows on the wall. "Wiggle your whiskers!" said Mamma. And what do you think Rolypoly saw?

The Talking Toy

Penny and Pickles had never been so bored. Mother Rabbit had asked them to watch Baby Honeybun while she went shopping.

"Don't leave her alone even for a moment," warned Mother. "Babies can get into all sorts of trouble before you know it. The time will fly by. Baby Honeybun is sure to keep you entertained."

But Baby Honeybun didn't do anything. First she slept for a long time, wiggling her little nose when Pickles leaned close to make sure she was still breathing.

"I thought babies cried all the time," said Penny, "but Baby Honeybun doesn't make a sound. I almost wish she would."

As if she had heard Penny, Baby Honeybun suddenly woke up and gave two big sneezes. They were such large sneezes coming from a tiny bunny that even Baby Honeybun herself looked shocked and shook her little whiskers to and fro.

"Maybe now she'll play with us," said Pickles. "Here, Baby! Chase Uncle Pickles!"

But Baby Honeybun just sat looking up at Pickles. She didn't move at all.

"Can she walk?" asked Pickles.

"I don't think so." Penny shook her head. "But I think she can roll around on her tummy."

"Well, she's not doing it now," said Pickles. "She's not doing anything at all. I didn't realize that babies were so boring. I bet I wasn't like this when I was little. Do something, Baby!"

Baby Honeybun blinked. She wiggled her nose. She gave a big sigh. And she went straight back to sleep, snuggled into a cushion on the floor.

Now anyone who has ever looked after a bunny baby – or any baby, for that matter – for any length of time will know that sleeping is a Good Thing. While a baby is sleeping, she isn't crawling into the coal scuttle or pulling off her clothes or doing any one of the hundreds of things that babies do so well.

But Penny didn't know much about babies, and that is why she made a Really Big Mistake. She nudged Baby Honeybun's toe to wake her up.

Baby Honeybun stirred, as though she didn't quite believe what she had felt.

Penny nudged her gently again.

Baby Honeybun opened one eye. There was no doubt about it.

She looked angry.

96

In fact, she looked angrier than any baby bunny Pickles and Penny had ever seen. Then Baby Honeybun opened her little pink mouth and began to yell.

It wasn't a quiet, unhappy kind of yell. It wasn't a medium-sized, slightly annoyed kind of yell. It was a huge, I-am-furious kind of yell, and it didn't stop.

Baby Honeybun yelled and yelled and yelled. Her little face grew pinker and pinker, and tiny tears ran down her furry cheeks.

"What should I do?" cried Penny. "I didn't mean to upset her!"

"Maybe she's hungry," suggested Pickles. "We could give her some milk." He always found a snack was helpful in a crisis.

"No, no," cried Penny. "She has a special kind and I don't know where it is. We don't want to poison her, too!"

"We could pick her up and cuddle her," suggested Pickles.

"You try," said Penny. "I'm not going to touch her again. Look what happened last time."

Very, very carefully, Pickles picked up the screaming baby. He was surprisingly heavy.

"Ouch!" yelled Pickles. And he put the baby back onto her cushion as quickly as he could.

"She kicked me!" he squealed.

"We'll have to try singing," said Penny. And she launched into a rousing chorus of "Five Little Bunnies" before Pickles could stop her. It didn't seem possible that Baby Honeybun could yell any louder, but she did. At the sound of the song, she made an extra-special effort, and her pink face went purple with rage.

Penny was almost in tears herself now. But she had no more ideas.

"We could tell her a story," said Pickles. "Once upon a time, there was a little baby bunny called Baby Honeybun. . . ."

Baby Honeybun's yells became a tiny fraction quieter.

". . . she lived in a burrow with her two best friends, Penny and Pickles," Penny went on.

Baby Honeybun's yells increased again.

"No, no, she didn't," said Pickles hastily. "She lived in a burrow with . . ."

Baby Honeybun threw her blue bunny toy across the room.

"She lived in a burrow with a cuddly blue bunny and . . ."

Baby Honeybun threw her pink butterfly rattle across the room.

". . . and a noisy pink butterfly," said Pickles, who was beginning to get the hang of this. "One day," he went on, "something really terrible happened to Baby Honeybun. She was left all alone with two big monsters, called Penny and Pickles. And they were *horrible*!"

Baby Honeybun stopped yelling for a moment and made a kind of gurgling noise. It was almost as if she was laughing.

"The horrible monsters did awful things," said Pickles. "They grabbed her and nearly dropped her. They made a terrible squeaky noise at her. And they woke her up when she was having a nice, quiet nap in the afternoon."

Baby Honeybun sighed again. For a whole two minutes she had forgotten to yell.

"The worst thing was," said Pickles, "that the monsters could not understand baby talk at all. This made Baby Honeybun so angry that all she could do was yell. Then she had a very good idea. She remembered that her cuddly blue bunny was able to speak lots of different languages, so she whispered in his ear what she wanted to say to the horrible monsters."

Pickles gently held the blue bunny close to Baby Honeybun. Then he held it up to his own furry ear.

"Is that so?" he asked, listening hard to the blue bunny. "Well, that is fine. Penny, please be quiet. Baby Honeybun wants to have a little nap."

And at that, Baby Honeybun gave a big yawn and closed her eyes.

When Mother Rabbit returned from her shopping a few minutes later, she found not one but *three* sleeping bunnies in her living room. And she was far too sensible to wake *any* of them.

Harold Hurbertus Bear

Harold Hurbertus Bear, HH to his friends, was no ordinary bear. His great grandmother had been a Princess among the royal Russian bears. His mother came from a long line of bears who had rubbed paws with Dukes and Countesses. In fact, he was a very well connected bear indeed.

HH was a kind bear and many people were fond of him, but he did tend to put on airs. "It just isn't proper to wear red in the morning," he would say, shaking his head, when he met another bear in the street. "Blue or grey only for the mornings, dear bear. We mustn't let standards drop."

In fact there was very little happening in Bearport that Harold Hurbertus didn't like to express an opinion about. "Of course, I am always consulted," he would say. "Other bears know that when it comes to matters of importance, you need a bear who has seen a bit of the world and mixed with the right people."

Now as far as anyone knew, Harold Hurbertus had only been as far as the seaside on a hot Saturday in the summer. It was true that he was sometimes invited to weddings and christenings of distant relations with titles to their names, but none had ever been seen visiting HH at Humpton Hall. This was what made it particularly annoying when Harold Hurbertus boasted about his friends. "As I was saying to the Duchess only the other day . . ." or "I know that Her Royal Highness agrees with me . . ." he would say.

"Its high time that bear came back down to earth," said Mr Bloomer the baker. "Any ideas, Basil?" Basil, his nephew, shook his head, but he looked thoughtful.

A few weeks later the whole town was buzzing with news. Princess Ursula Berelli was coming to visit Harold Hurbertus.

"Is she a relative of yours?" Mr Bloomer asked HH.

"Er. . . well, I believe . . . er . . . ours is a

rather big family, you know," said HH. "She's a rather distant . . . er . . . cousin, I think."

Harold Hurbertus worked night and day to make sure the visit would be a success. He had several rooms in the Hall redecorated and six extra gardeners working on the lawns, just in case the Princess wanted to take a stroll.

At the agreed time, Harold Hurbertus had all the servants line up at the steps of the Hall. A very small car swept through the gates and up to the front door.

When the car door opened, out stepped someone who was undoubtedly a Princess. Well, she wore a little crown on her head.

"My dear Princess," murmered HH, has your car broken down?"

The Princess roared with laughter. "You dear old fashioned thing!" she shrieked. "Nobody who is *anybody* is driving a large car nowadays. Think of the environment, Humblebus."

"Quite so, quite so," said her host. "It's Harold Hurbertus, actually. Won't you come into the Hall?"

105

The Princess allowed herself to be led into the dining room, where the tables were piled high with a range of dishes. The Princess allowed her eyes to linger for a minute on a particularly fine looking dessert before she said, "Dear Horribilus, I'm afraid I never touch anything richer than a slice of toast and a morsel of cheese. Why not give this wonderful food to the people of the town?"

"What a charming idea," said HH with a gulp. "I'll tell the servants to take it away at once. And . . . er . . . it's Harold Hurbertus."

"A thousand apologies, Hardboiledus," cried the Princess. "But tell me, are you really so behind the times as to have servants? I can hardly believe it."

106

"Er . . . that sort of thing is no longer done, I suppose, in your circle?" enquired HH in a shaky voice.

"Goodness me no, Hurglegurglus," laughed the Princess. "I'm sure, like me, that you would prefer to do your own cooking and cleaning. It's so much more modern."

It was not until the end of a long and very tiring day, after the Princess had forced Harold Hurbertus to carry plates of food to every inhabitant of Bearport, that HH noticed that the Princess was wearing a bracelet that quite clearly read, *Basil*.

As HH walked home, old and young bears stopped to shake his hand and thank him for his generosity.

"I fear," said Harold Hurbertus to himself, "that I have been a very foolish bear. But everyone else is happy and that makes me happy too. And only a bear with real pedigree can take a joke as well as I can after all."

Farmer Barnes' Spring Clean

Farmer Barnes does like things to be clean, and on a busy farm that's pretty difficult. So that is why, once a year, Farmer Barnes has his big Spring Clean. Everything gets cleaned, from the cupboard under the sink to the roof of Biggy Pig's sty.

You've never seen so much washing and brushing, dusting and polishing. All the animals join in.

The last stage of the Spring Clean takes place in the farmhouse. Farmer Barnes carries all the furniture out into the yard and vacuums the house from top to bottom. Then he carries the tables and chairs and beds back into the house and plonks himself down on the sofa. Spring Cleaning is over for another year.

But this year, as Farmer Barnes cleaned furiously, something dreadful happened. It started to rain! Not just a little gentle shower, but pouring down, splashing on the table and making puddles on the chairs.

"He'll be cross," said Busy Hen anxiously, sheltering under a stool.

"He'll shout and stomp about," agreed Mrs. Speckles. "I don't want to be around when that starts."

Then, as suddenly as it began, the rain stopped.

A few minutes later, Farmer Barnes appeared in the yard. He looked at the soggy furniture. His face went red. His forehead furrowed. The animals waited for the second storm of the day.

Then the farmer began to laugh. "This is the cleanest my furniture has ever been," he roared. "Let's hope this happens every year!"

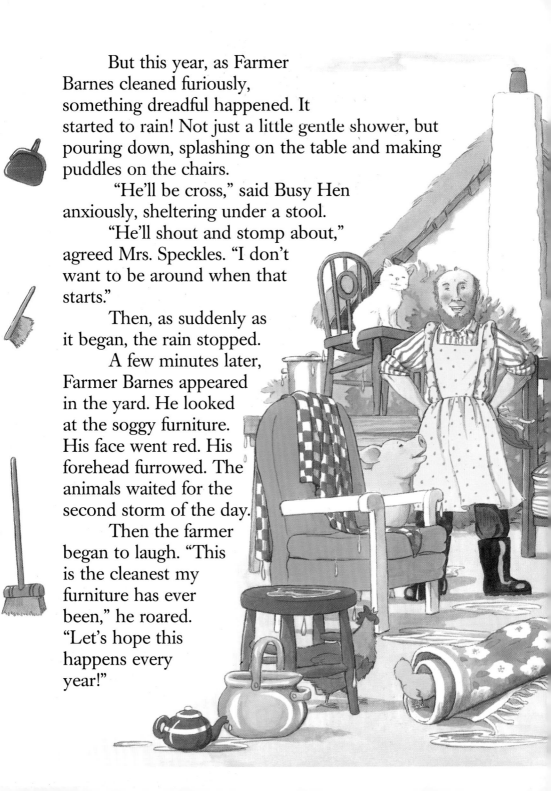

A Very Odd Feeling

Puppies, as I'm sure you know, can be
naughtier than almost any other little animals.
They chew things. They sharpen their little claws
on things. And when they are very small, I'm afraid
they sometimes leave little . . . er . . . *puddles* around
the place. You can imagine that teaching a whole
class of puppies is not an easy job. Mr Terrier the
Teacher felt that he needed five pairs of paws and
eyes in the back of his head.

One morning, when Mr Terrier took off his
hat and began to write on the board about the
important subject of lampposts and how to use them,
he heard a lot of giggling going on at the back of
the room.

"Ruffles! Rupert! Randall! Is that you?" he called, knowing that the naughty triplets were often at the bottom of any trouble. But the three little dogs spoke up at once with solemn faces.

"No, sir!"
"No, sir!"
"No, sir!"

Mr Terrier frowned and turned back to his writing. But now the giggling was louder than ever. Mr Terrier spun around as quickly as he could, his ears flying. In fact, he turned so quickly he felt dizzy and had to clutch at his desk. He was not quick enough. As the room revolved gently around him, all the poor teacher could see was twenty innocent little faces looking up at him. Slowly, he turned back to his work.

This time, the giggling was uncontrolled. When Mr Terrier turned around, he saw little puppies rolling on the floor with merriment. Some even had tears of laughter dripping from their whiskers.

Mr Terrier used his iciest tones.

"Would someone please tell me just *what* is so funny? Well? *Oooooh*!"

Just at that moment, Mr Terrier felt a very odd feeling where his shirt collar met his neck. It was slithery and slimy and squirmy and enough to make even the bravest dog run yelping to his mother. Mr Terrier would have done just that if it were not for the fact that twenty pairs of naughty eyes were watching him eagerly. And twenty pink tongues were panting with glee.

"Rupert!" called the teacher. "Would you come here a minute, please?" It took all Mr Terrier's self-control not to start squealing.

Rupert trotted to the front of the class, looking a little apprehensive.

"I wonder," said Mr Terrier, "if you would mind removing the snake that is wriggling down my neck. I wouldn't want it to get squashed."

Mr Terrier was determined to remain cool and calm. It would take more than a slithering reptile to frighten *him*.

Rupert looked puzzled.

"There isn't a snake wriggling down your neck, sir," he said. "No snake at all."

"Well, the lizard then," said Mr Terrier, feeling more uncomfortable by the second, but determined not to show it. "Don't split hairs with me, young puppy."

"There's no lizard either, sir," said Rupert looking horribly truthful.

"Is it a spider? Is it a worm? Is it a centipede?" asked Mr Terrier, his voice rising with every question. Then he had an even worse thought. "Is it," he squeaked, "a frog?"

"Sir, are you feeling well?" asked Rupert, looking concerned. "Why don't you sit down? It is hot in here."

Mr Terrier could feel the slithering and sliding getting worse and worse. He simply couldn't bear it any more. Visions of tarantulas, toads, and things that crawl out from under rocks filled his head. He gave a little cry and pulled off his coat, flinging it on the floor.

From out of the coat, something red and yellow and slimy began to crawl.

Mr Terrier stepped back in horror. Was it some alien life form, ready to take over the world?

But as he looked, horrified, at the horrible stuff, Mr Terrier's nose began to twitch. When a dog's eyes are playing tricks on him, his nose will often set him straight. And this time, Mr Terrier's nose was telling him something very strange. It was telling him that the slimy yellow and red crawling stuff was . . . plums and custard!

Mr Terrier took a step forward. He looked carefully at the mess on the floor. It smelled like plums and custard. It looked like plums and custard. Mr Terrier stooped down and put out a cautious paw. He raised the paw to his mouth. There was no doubt about it, it was plums and custard! Lots of it!

Mr Terrier was angry. He was very angry indeed. Wiping the back of his neck with his handkerchief as best he could, he faced the class.

"Which of you naughty, nasty, *silly* little puppies have done this?" he asked. "And," he went on, as a thought struck him, "how?"

Mr Terrier looked at the ceiling for a hanging bucket of dripping custard. There wasn't one.

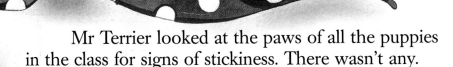

Mr Terrier looked at the paws of all the puppies in the class for signs of stickiness. There wasn't any.

Mr Terrier looked under desks and inside schoolbags for spoons or bowls or cartons. There weren't any.

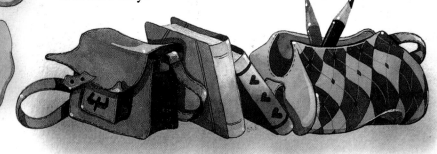

And then, at the back of Mr Terrier's mind, there came a little whispering thought. It told him his elderly mother had been making supper last night. It told him she had been pouring something into a big bowl. It told him that, as he handed her the telephone, he had also put his hat down on the table. It also told him he had rushed to work this morning without stopping to think about anything, even the slightly strange way his hat felt as it sat on his head.

"Puppies!" said Mr Terrier. "I owe you an apology. I know now that you did not put snakes or lizards, or worms, or frogs, or tarantulas, or plums and custard on my head or down my back. The culprit . . . and I will not hesitate to name him . . . was . . . ME! Sometimes old dogs can be as silly as young ones. Now I must go and clean myself up."

And it is an even stranger thing that all those puppies liked Mr Terrier a lot more after that, and they were never as naughty again.

The Rainy Day

Mrs. Millie Mouse looked out of the window at the rain "Poor Daphne!" Mr. Mouse knew exactly what she meant. His wife's sister Daphne was getting married and he had heard of little else for weeks.

Mrs. Mouse put on her raincoat and hat and hurried out into the rain. She needed to visit her friends to discuss the dreadful calamity. They had to decide what to do with the mountains of food they had all been preparing. And what about the amazingly huge hats they had all made, each trying to outdo the other?

Mrs. Mouse found all her friends at Mrs. Martha Mouse's large house.

"I'd love to offer to have the wedding here," cried Mrs. Martha Mouse, "but there isn't room for three hundred guests."

"Underground, maybe?" queried Millie Mouse.

"Oh no! It would be so dark and cramped. And my hat won't fit any of the passages!"

Now you may notice that we have not yet met Daphne and her fiancé Tom. As a matter of fact, neither of them wanted all this fuss, which had been arranged entirely by the mouse ladies without stopping to ask if it was wanted at all.

While the ladies chattered, and the rain poured down, the two mice who should have been more worried than anyone, were smiling happily. Their dream of a quiet wedding had come true after all as they stood beneath a young oak tree with only the Reverend Alfred Mouse for company.

"I love the rain," whispered Daphne, "don't you?"

"Almost as much," whispered Tom, "as I love you."

The Bear With Bells

Let me introduce myself. I'm Hermann P. Bear from Switzerland. No, I don't know what the P. stands for, I'm afraid. Now with all respect, I've found that today's bears are just as brave and clever as the noble bears of yesterday. My story proves just that. And it didn't happen so very long ago, either.

This story concerns a friend of mine, back home among the mountains. I'll call him Fritz. That is not his real name, but he is a modest bear and, if he ever appears in public again, he would not want the world to know the part he played in the Great Zurich Bank Robbery.

Now Fritz is the cleverest, kindest, jolliest bear you could ever hope to meet, but since the day he was sewn, he has suffered a great hardship. Around his neck, his toymaker has put a collar of jingling, jangling, clinking, clanking, ting-a-linging tiny bells.

I can see how horrified you are to hear this. Yes, poor Fritz could not creep off to see his friends during the night. He could not stretch his legs during the day, in case his owner heard him. He was forced to sit quite still, hour after hour, for fear of revealing the great secret of bearness.

Now Fritz was such an unusual bear that he was bought by a collector. Yes, a grown-up person who had over a hundred very beautiful bears. I myself . . . *ahem* . . . was one of them. The grown-up was a very rich gentleman, who, in all honesty, cared more about money than bears. He loved us for the francs (that's Swiss money) we were worth, not for the very fine bears we all were.

One day, this gentleman went to America to buy some bears. While he was gone, he put all his dearest possessions in the bank, and that included some of us bears. It was dreadful. We were kept in a trunk in a large safe-deposit box, where a bear only had to move a whisker to set off dozens of alarms and sirens. I soon learned to admire Fritz even more. Imagine living like that all the time!

We had been living in the bank for two long weeks, when the Great Robbery took place. Of course, we realised very little, inside our trunk. We heard the explosion and felt ourselves being jiggled about as the trunk was carried out, but we only guessed what had happened, as we could see very little through the keyhole of the trunk.

It was some hours later, in a cold Swiss dawn, that the robbers arrived at their hideaway - a cave tucked away in the side of a mountain. They hid their truck among some trees nearby and set about dividing up their ill-gotten gains.

All went well as they opened the boxes which contained jewels and gold coins. Then the lid of our trunk was roughly opened and a very unpleasant man peered inside.

I'm afraid that the language he used when he saw us sitting there was quite unrepeatable. My ears turned quite pink, I can tell you. The stupid man had no idea we were valuable bears at all.

He kicked the trunk so hard it toppled over, and we fell onto the cold floor of the cave, with icicles dripping down on us. My fur has never been the same ever since.

It was almost dark when we heard noises outside. It was the police! They had followed the tracks of the robbers' truck to the nearby trees. Now the cave was very well hidden. All the robbers had to do was to keep still.

"There was probably a helicopter waiting," I heard a policeman say. "They won't be here now." Now, as you know, humans cannot hear bear speech, so we were unable to make a noise, but Fritz was a very brave bear indeed. He jumped to his feet and began to jingle and jangle as hard as he could. Every bell around his neck was clinking and clanking. In this silence, it seemed to be an enormous noise. The most vicious looking of the robbers - and none of them looked angelic - leaped towards Fritz with a murderous cry. At that moment, a powerful flashlight lit the dramatic scene.

Well, the rest is history. The robbers were caught, the loot was recovered, and the bears were taken into custody as evidence. None of the humans realised whom they had to thank, of course. But then, we all know that they do not have our education. Eventually, we were sold to new owners, all over the world.

And Fritz? Well, I can't be sure. He fell behind a boulder and was not found with the rest of us. There are sometimes stories of strange tinkling, jingling sounds to be heard in the mountains, as though a bear with bells around his neck might be skidding happily down the slopes. One or two people have found strange paw prints in the snow. I hope that Fritz is happy, living the life of a free and furry bear.

But if you should ever find yourselves in danger in the Alps, dear friends, you might call out the name of Hermann P. Bear. I like to think that a very old friend of mine would come to your aid.

Mother Bear's Problem

One morning, Mother Bear had a worried look on her furry face. "I know there is something I'm supposed to remember about today," she said, "but I can't for the life of me think what it is."

"It's my birthday!" suggested Barney hopefully.

"It's *your* birthday!" Barney was trying to help.

"I think I'd remember my own birthday Barney," said Mother Bear coldly. "I may have forgotten one little thing, but I haven't completely lost my senses."

But Mother Bear was still worried. She checked her calendar to make sure that it wasn't time for her dentist's appointment, or Barney's school concert, or Mr Bear's fishing contest. She went through her papers to make sure that her bills were paid. Still she knew that she had not remembered the thing she had forgotten.

By half-past three, Mother Bear and her husband were settled on the sofa with mugs of coffee, a box of chocolates and wearing their oldest comfiest slippers.

The film was so exciting that Mother Bear almost forgot about her problem, until there came a ring at the doorbell.

"Hello, darlings!" called Aunt Hortense, opening the door herself. "I've come to stay until Monday as I promised," she exclaimed.

"I've remembered what I forgot," groaned Mother Bear to Mr Bear, too softly for Aunt Hortense to hear. "I was going to suggest that we all went away for the weekend!"

Sweet Dreams, Harold!

When you have a warm, dry stable, filled with fresh, golden straw, and your tummy is full of oats and carrots and other good things, you should be able to get a good night's sleep – if you're a horse, of course! But poor old Harold Horse spent all day dozing in the sun.

"It's because I can't get a wink of sleep at night," he told Busy Hen.

"Why not?" asked Busy Hen. "You've got a lovely stable. It's much nicer than our henhouse. I've often told Cackle."

"It's not that," yawned Harold. "It's the noise at night. It's terrible!"

Cackle started to strut about. "I do not make a noise in the night," he crowed. "I wait until it's almost, almost daybreak. I do! I do!"

"Nobody said it was you, Cackle," clucked Busy Hen. "Your crowing is beautiful.

I believe it's those mice. Am I right, Harold?"

"Quite right," agreed the old horse. "They are scritch-scratching all night long. Some noises can be ignored – like the wind in the trees, or the rain on the roof. But you can't ignore scritch-scratching. You just can't."

"Leave it to me," said Busy Hen. And later in the day she went to Harold's stable and had a very long conversation with a little person with a twitchety nose and a long tail.

A week later, Harold was trotting about the farmyard as usual, much to everyone's delight. And Busy Hen was as proud as punch of the brand new henhouse she shared with Cackle and the other hens.

"I knew Farmer Barnes wouldn't leave us in that old henhouse once it had mice in it," she clucked. "And those mice just love their new home – so everyone's happy!"

133

Too Much Fudge

One afternoon, Pickles and Penny didn't feel very well. In fact, they felt so sick that their ears and whiskers drooped and they went to bed – while the sun was still shining.

Mother Rabbit was worried about her little ones. She asked them all kinds of questions about what might be wrong.

"Have you got colds?" she inquired. "Are there sniffles in your noses?"

"No, Mother," groaned Pickles.

"Did you play in the hot sun without your hats on? Are your ears aching?"

"No, Mother," moaned Penny.

"I may have to call Doctor Baggins," said Mother, "if you two don't feel better soon. I'll just go and get you each a glass of water."

But in the kitchen, Mother Rabbit saw something that made her change her mind about calling the doctor, and she didn't look quite so worried when she went back to the little rabbits.

"I'll just sit here and tell you a story," said Mother Rabbit, "and you can go to sleep and feel much better when you wake up."

"Once upon a time," said Mother Rabbit, "there were two little rabbits who always did what their mother told them. They were as good as gold. They wouldn't dream of hiding under the bed when it was time to wash the dishes. They always squeezed the toothpaste from the end of the tube. They never left dirty pawmarks in the bathroom. It was always a pleasure for their mother to look at her two little rabbits and say, 'My children are not silly like other bunnies. They are good, sensible young rabbits.'"

While Mother Rabbit was talking, quite a bit of wriggling and jiggling could be heard coming from two little bunnies in bed. Mother Rabbit smiled grimly.

"One day," she went on, "the little rabbits' mother was very busy in the kitchen. There was a Grand Fair the next day, and she had promised to bake some cakes for the cake stall. But when she looked in her cupboard, she found that she didn't have any eggs. She had no time to run out and buy some more, so she looked at the ingredients she did have to see if there was something else she could make. Pretty soon, she was melting all kinds of good things in a pan. A lovely smell came out of the kitchen, so that the two little rabbits came to see what was being cooked. The mother rabbit was stirring something with a big wooden spoon.

'This fudge isn't for you!' she laughed."

137

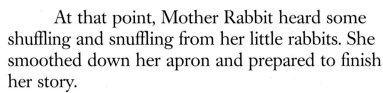

At that point, Mother Rabbit heard some shuffling and snuffling from her little rabbits. She smoothed down her apron and prepared to finish her story.

"By lunchtime," she said, "the mother rabbit had filled ten large tins with hot fudge. She put the pans on the kitchen table to cool. Of course, she knew that her little ones would never dream of tasting the delicious fudge. They knew that they must not eat sweet, sticky things between meals. So you can imagine how surprised she was when she came back from hanging out the laundry to find that two of the pans of fudge were missing. Obviously, she thought, someone had believed that she would not be able to count so many pans and might not notice that some were gone."

Now there was a deep silence from the two little rabbits. Mother Rabbit decided it was time to finish her story.

"Of course," she said, "it was very easy for the mother rabbit to find out who had stolen the fudge. Any rabbit would feel ill after eating a whole pan of sweet, sticky stuff. All she had to do was to visit all her friends and see who was looking a bit green around the whiskers. By the way, how are you two little bunnies feeling now? Any better? Or do I need to call Dr. Baggins?"

"No, no," cried Pickles and Penny, creeping out of their beds. "There's nothing wrong with us at all now. We feel fine!"

But you know, it's a strange thing, neither of those two little rabbits wanted anything for supper!

Too Many Princesses!

Sometimes it is nice to feel special. Of course, in lots of ways, everyone in the world is special, and it may not be a very good thing that some Princesses feel they are more special than other people. The reason they feel this is simply that there are not many Princesses about – except in Coronel, that is.

For the Kingdom of Coronel has more Princesses to the square mile than any other country in the world. The reasons for this are very complicated. You would need to read six books about royal family trees to understand it. Even most of the people of Coronel don't understand quite why there are so many Princesses about. All they know is that it is best to call a lady you have never met before "Your Highness" just in case. If she is a Princess, you have done the right thing. If not, no harm has been done.

Now, you might think that Princesses, who often feel lonely in their great castles and grand palaces, would be glad to find lots of other Princesses to be friends with. Well, some of them do, but one in particular was not pleased at all.

The Princess I am thinking of was called Melinda. She grew up in a castle in the kingdom next to Coronel, far up in the mountains. Melinda had no brothers or sisters. She was also, I'm afraid, not very fond of reading. That is why, until the time that she was a big girl of twelve, she believed she was the only Princess in the world.

I mentioned that Melinda did not like reading. In fact, she did not like any kind of learning very much. Her geography was dreadful. Her history was even worse. And as for her mathematics! It was just as well that she had so many servants to help her, for she would never have managed to add up the money in her money box herself.

Although the Princess was perfectly happy, her father the King was not. He knew that one day she might have to take charge of the castle and all the people that lived there, and he was very much afraid she would be too silly to do it properly.

One day, Melinda's father called her to him. "My dear," he said, "it is time you went to school. There is a great deal you need to learn, and it is time you made some friends among girls of your own age."

Princess Melinda did not feel very enthusiastic about going to school, but she was sometimes a little lonely, so when the day came, she set off happily for Coronel.

When Princess Melinda arrived at her school, the headmistress showed her to her room, which she was to share with another girl. Melinda had never shared a room before, but she thought to herself that it would be useful to have someone to clean her shoes and keep her clothes looking nice. She was very much surprised when the girl, whose name was Siska, did not seem to notice Melinda's trunk needed to be unpacked.

After ten minutes, Melinda could bear it no longer. "My clothes will be crushed and ruined," she complained, "if you don't see to them straight away."

Siska looked puzzled. "Why should I see to them?" she asked. "They're your clothes."

Melinda was so stunned she could hardly speak. "B-b-b-because I'm a *Princess*!"

"Well, so am I," replied Siska calmly. "So are most of the girls in the school."

If Melinda was stunned before, she was now so shocked she collapsed onto her bed in a heap!

Another Princess? Lots of other Princesses? She felt as if her whole world was turning upside down. What was the point of being a Princess if everybody was one? It was truly dreadful.

Over the next few days, things went from bad to worse for Melinda. Not only were most of the other girls Princesses, but most of them were cleverer, prettier and more popular than she was. Melinda found she wasn't nearly as special as she had always thought. And it was not a very pleasant feeling.

Perhaps it was because she was not very happy that Melinda began to pay more attention at school. She started to read more, too. When the other girls chatted about how many diamonds they had in their coronets, Melinda had her nose in a book, learning about how coronets are made. When the other girls went dancing with the Princes at the school down the road, Melinda read a book about the history of ballrooms.

Gradually, she grew happier, until the day came when she no longer cared whether she was a Princess or not.

When Melinda was almost grown–up, the time came for her to leave school and return home. She was a very different girl.

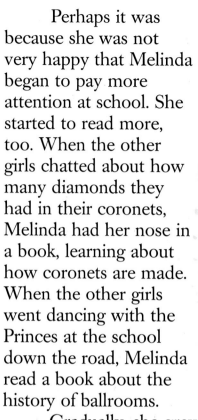

Her father was delighted to see how sensible and capable she had become. Over supper, Melinda outlined her plans for repairing the castle. As she went off to bed, she mentioned her ideas for improving the way the royal lands were farmed. At breakfast the next day, she thought of a brilliant way to make the work of the portcullis–keeper much easier. The King beamed at her across the table. "My dear," he said, "I am old and tired.

No, don't say anything! It is true. Now I can do something I have longed to do for a long time. I shall no longer be King. You will rule in my place, and I know that you will do it wisely and well. You are a very special girl indeed."

Melinda was just about to protest that she was not special at all, for there were many, many clever and accomplished Princesses, when a thought struck her. When she ruled the kingdom, she would no longer be a Princess. She would be a Queen – and there really are not very many of those in the world at all. Melinda smiled and kissed her father. There really is something very *special* about being special.

The Ghostly Bear

Little bears, the story I am about to tell you is very, very scary. If you get frightened, you must put your paws over your ears and cuddle up to a grown-up bear.

When I was a very little bear myself, my aunty told me this tale. She was a very sensible bear, so I am sure that every word is true.

Once upon a time, in a faraway land, there was a huge castle. It was tall and dark. Vines covered the turrets and many of the dusty windows. Bats fluttered from the battlements.

The castle stood empty for many years, but one day there was great excitement in the nearby village. It was said that the owner of the castle was coming to visit. Now no one had ever seen this mysterious owner, so there was a great deal of talk about who it might be.

"I've heard it is a countess," said the baker. "She was once a great beauty. Then a witch put a curse on her. Since then she has always worn a veil to hide her ugly face."

"No, no," replied the blacksmith, "the owner *is* a witch. She travels at night, and has a black cat."

"Nonsense!" said the school teacher waving her stick. "It is simply an old woman who cannot move around very well. That is why she has not visited for a long time."

Every day, the children in the village looked out for the important visitor, but no one came along the winding road from the forest. Then, one morning, a little girl called Lucy noticed smoke rising above the highest tower in the castle.

"She must have come in the night!" she called to everyone she met. "She is a witch after all."

When they heard this, the villagers were very worried. "We must take her a big present," they said, "so she does not get angry with us. Who knows what spells she may cast if she feels we are unfriendly."

That seemed to be a good idea, so a collection was made and a beautiful chest was bought to be given to the witch (if that is what she was).

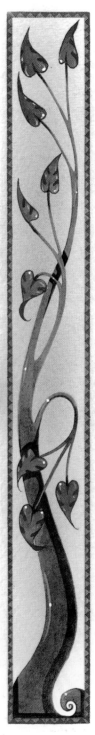

"Now," said the baker, "who will give the present to the witch? I cannot go with my weak heart and that long, winding path to climb."

"Nor can I," said the teacher, "with my bad leg."

For one reason or another, not one of the grown-ups in the village could deliver the present to the mysterious visitor.

"I'll go," said Lucy. "I'd like to see what she looks like."

"But," said the blacksmith, "won't you be frightened?"

"Oh no," replied Lucy. "I will take my teddy bear with me. He'll keep me safe."

She certainly was a very sensible little girl.

That afternoon, Lucy set off to the castle, carrying her bear and the chest. It was a long climb up the winding path, but at last she stood before the doors of the castle and knocked.

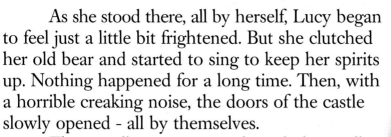

As she stood there, all by herself, Lucy began to feel just a little bit frightened. But she clutched her old bear and started to sing to keep her spirits up. Nothing happened for a long time. Then, with a horrible creaking noise, the doors of the castle slowly opened - all by themselves.

There really was not much to do but walk straight in, and Lucy was beginning to feel that anything was better than standing on the doorstep.

She found herself in a great, dark hall. The ceiling was so high the little girl could not see the top of it. At the far end of the room, a figure in a dark cloak was crouched on a chair as large as a throne.

It wore a hood, so Lucy could not see its face, but a long, bony finger beckoned her.

155

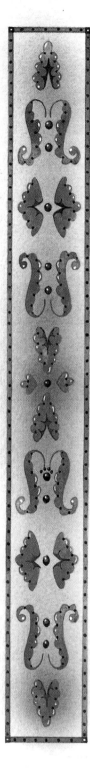

When the little girl was standing in front of the finger at last, she tried to speak up bravely, though there was a quiver in her voice.

"Please, your highness, or your witchness, we all wanted to welcome you to the castle and give you this present."

A horrible cackle came from the dark-robed figure. "A chest? I've got hundreds of them," it croaked. "But I can see that you do have one thing I want. Give me that teddy bear, and I will let you go home safely."

"No!" cried Lucy, hugging her teddy bear. "You can't have him."

"Really?" the voice replied. "Then I shall have to lock you up until you agree."

The next thing Lucy knew, she was being dragged into a room which contained an enormous four poster bed, and the door of the room was being locked behind her.

Lucy stayed in the room until it began to get dark. Then the dark figure brought her some food and a single candle.

"Go to bed," it said. "Let's see if you feel so brave in the morning."

Lucy climbed into bed and pulled the covers up to her chin. She felt more frightened than she had ever felt in her life, but somehow, she managed to go to sleep.

158

At midnight, she was awoken by a clock clanging loudly near her bed.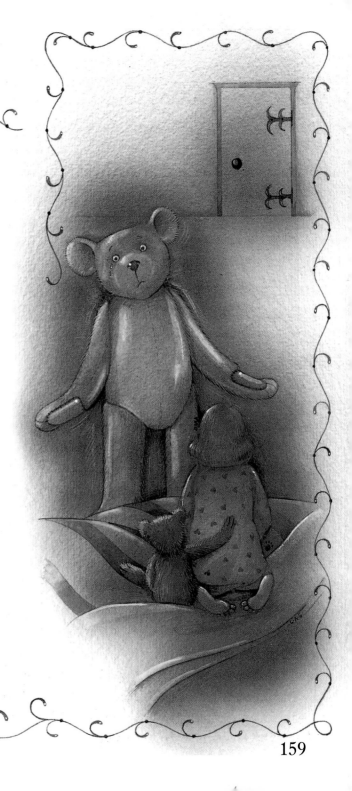

Dong! Dong! Dong!

She woke to find a large, white bear standing by her bed. He seemed to be shimmering with a strange light.

"W . . . w . . . what do you want?" she asked.

The strange bear said nothing but it held out its furry paws toward Lucy's little bear, tucked up beside her in bed.

"No!" cried Lucy. "He's mine!"

But then she saw an extraordinary thing. Large crystal tears were running down the shining bears face and dripping onto the little girl's bed.

He looked so very sad that Lucy could not bear it. "All right," she said quietly. "Don't be sad. Here's my own special bear to cheer you up." And she handed her own teddy bear to the strange, ghostly visitor. With a sigh, holding the little bear gently in his arms, the shining bear turned away. Lucy watched as he walked toward the door . . . and melted straight through it! Lucy shut her eyes and rubbed them. When she opened them, she was back in her own room, tucked up in her own little bed. Only her teddy bear was missing.

Next morning, the whole village gathered in amazement at the foot of the hill. Overnight, the castle had changed in an extraordinary way. The windows were sparkling. The vine had been cut. There were flags flying from the turrets and white doves fluttering around the battlements.

161

"It must have been bewitched after all," gasped the villagers.

"Our act of kindness in sending the chest has broken the spell. That is often the way in old stories."

Lucy thought about what had happened. She thought about the chest hidden under her bed.

"Someone was very unhappy," she thought. "And now they are not. That is what bears are for."

I believe she was right, my friends. The mystery never was solved. Later it was said that the Countess who lived in the castle had suffered an unhappy childhood. Perhaps returning to the castle of her birth had brought a smile to her face again. Only Lucy had a different idea.

By the Light of the Moon

Faraway on the top of the world, there is a place that is always cold, with white snow and the icy sea. There are no trees and no flowers at all. There are only seals and fish and bears. And when those polar bears are about, the seals and the fish need to watch out, because those bears can creep ever so quietly…

and slide ever so slippily…

and run ever so quickly…

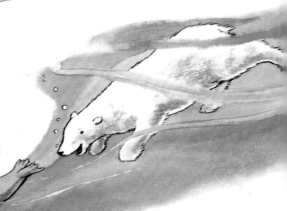

and dive down into the deep blue sea with hardly a splash, when they are looking for a snack.

"I love being a polar bear!" one little bear told his mother once. "The sun shines

all the time and makes the snow sparkle."

"Well, that is true," said his mother, "but you are only a little bear and have not yet been alive for a whole year. In the summer the sun shines all the time, even at night. But in the winter, the sun doesn't shine at all. Not even in the daytime."

The little bear went away to a cosy ice cave to think. And the more he thought, the more he felt very, very sad. The long, dark winter was coming, and it would be too dark to play and swim and slide.

One night, the little bear noticed that everything around him was deep blue and velvety.

"The sun has gone away until next year," said his mother. "It is winter now."

The little bear looked around. The snow was shining with a silvery light. It was the moon!

The little bear gave a sigh. There was nothing to fear. In the summer and the winter, he still lived in a wonderful world.

Why Am I Blue?

Once upon a time, there was a little blue elephant. Little Blue lived with his family on a dusty plain, munching and marching, marching and munching.

One day, the elephants came to a waterhole that was not as muddy as usual. It had clear, clean water, sparkling in the sunshine. Mother Elephant ushered Little Blue to the front. She didn't want him to be left behind. The little elephant looked down. Another little elephant looked back at him.

It was the first time that Little Blue had seen his reflection. It was wonderful!

It was only when he was full of the clear, clean water that the little elephant turned to his mother and asked, "Why am I blue?" He could see now that none of the other elephants looked at all like him.

"You are blue because blue is right for you," Little Blue's mother replied.

But Little Blue felt strange and different. Then, one day, far away across the plain, he saw a wonderful sight. Pink, yellow and, yes, blue elephants were strolling along just ahead. Without a second thought, Little Blue scampered to meet them. He felt so happy to see other grown-up elephants who looked just like him. "I shall stay with these friendly elephants," he said.

But that night, as he tried to sleep under the stars, Little Blue realized he didn't really belong with the strange elephants. Under the huge moon, he trotted back to his own family.

"I'm so glad you're back, Little Blue," whispered his mother, sleepily.

"Mother, I like being blue," he whispered back. "Blue is just right."

"And you are just right, too," said his mother. "Now go to sleep, Little Blue. All elephants need their rest, even blue ones."

Bedtime for Little Bears

All little bears love to snuggle down in their beds at night and go to sleep. But before they go to bed, little bears must have their baths, and some little bears just do not like to get their ears wet!

Once there was a little bear called Barney, who really hated his bath. His father tried everything to make bathtime fun. A huge boat and a bottle of the biggest bubbles you have ever seen didn't work. Three yellow ducks, a water wheel, and some stuff that turned the water purple didn't work either.

One day, Barney went for a walk with his granny. As they walked, it started to rain. Right away, Barney started to complain.

"I don't like getting wet," he whined. "It gets in my ears and in my eyes and up my nose, and it's horrible."

"Well, Barney, I am surprised," said Granny, "that you would want to give up all that good luck. Don't you know it's lucky for a little bear to get wet?"

The next night at bathtime, Barney's father was surprised to find that Barney jumped right into the tub with no fuss at all. And these days Barney is the luckiest little bear you have ever met – and the cleanest!

The Best Birthday

When it was almost time for Pickles' birthday,
nobody had any peace. Pickles was determined to
have the biggest and best birthday that had ever been
seen in Warren Wood. But what should it be like?
Ever since he had been to Billy Bunny's Pirate Party,
Pickles felt that a party should have a theme. He just
couldn't decide what his should be.

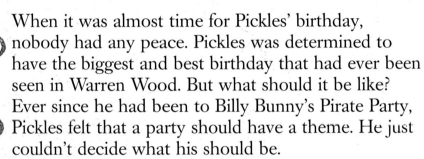

"How about Dragons and Princesses?" Penny
asked, who fancied the
idea of dressing up as a
beautiful princess.

"I don't want to be
a dragon," said Pickles.

"How about Fairies
and Elves?" suggested
Penny. A fairy costume
would be good, too.

"My ears are large
enough without
pretending to be an elf,"

replied Pickles. "And anyway, Jimble already had one of those for his birthday last year. It would look as if I was copying."

Every day, Pickles worried about his party.

He was still worrying a few days later, when Cousin Hoppity came to stay.

Cousin Hoppity lived in a wood that was even wilder than Warren Wood and had a large river flowing through it. He was always full of stories of the adventures he had had. Pickles secretly envied him, but he always pretended to enjoy the calmer life under the oak tree. "When it comes to birthdays," said Cousin Hoppity, "I'm the rabbit you want to ask. On my very best birthday, I didn't even *have* a party."

Despite himself, Pickles heard his own voice asking to hear the story. Hoppity was only too glad to begin.

171

"My birthday is in the spring," he said, "when the river is always high and fast-flowing. Last year, it rained for days and days and days. On the morning of my birthday, I woke up to a splashing sound."

"Rain on the window?" asked Pickles in a bored voice.

"Water on the window, certainly," said Hoppity, "but it was lapping at the panes, not falling on them. The whole wood was flooded, right up to the second branch of our tree."

Penny was horrified. "What about all the poor rabbits underground?" she cried.

"Rabbits in Wilderness Wood are sensible and strong," said Hoppity. "They had all climbed up into the trunk of the tree and were busy making boats out of everything they could find. As I looked out of the window, my great-grandmother sailed past in a suitcase. She had made a sail out of an old pair of her . . . ahem, well, bloomers."

The little rabbits all giggled at the idea, but Pickles had more questions.

"What happened to all your presents?" he asked. He was thinking about the interesting packages that he knew were hiding under his parents' bed at that very moment.

"Luckily," said Hoppity, "they were the kind of presents that float. One by one, they came floating past my window, and I fished them out with my fishing rod. It was loads of fun, even if some of them were pretty soggy for a while. And my birthday cake never was seen again."

173

"I can see that it was exciting," said Pickles. "But why was it the best birthday ever?"

"Because of the whale," cried Hoppity, stretching his paws out wide. "A great big whale swam up the river and into the wood, and it got stuck between two trees."

Pickles was almost speechless. "A w-w-whale?" he gasped. "In Wilderness Wood? What happened to it?"

"We all made boats of everything we could find," said Hoppity, "as I explained. Then we sailed out and attached ropes to the whale. It was a tough job, but at last we were able to pull him out from between the trees and tow him back to the river and, eventually, the sea. It was the adventure of a lifetime, I can assure you. I can't imagine that anything as exciting as that happens in Warren Wood, does it?"

Pickles and Penny were silent. Nothing they had ever heard of even came close. It made the Party Problem seem pathetically small.

It was only later that night that Pickles began to think hard about that whale.

The next morning, he tackled Hoppity. "There wasn't really a whale, was there?" he asked with a smile.

"Of course not," laughed Hoppity, "but it was a really good story, wasn't it? Now, what about a Deep Sea Party for your birthday?"

Pickles had to admit that was a pretty good idea. And Penny was as happy as could be, as she planned her mermaid costume.

The Sniffles

Bobby Bunny was getting ready to go out to play when his mother called him back.

"You need your scarf on a day like this," she said. "We don't want you catching the sniffles, do we?"

Bobby was puzzled. "How do Sniffles look?" he asked.

"Droopy ears, a red nose, and wiggly whiskers," grunted his father.

Bobby ran out to play with his friends. He had a wonderful time. The sun was already beginning to go down when he set off home.

The trees made dark shadows on the lane as Bobby scuttled along. He suddenly began to think about the Sniffles. Just then, there was a swooshing noise in a nearby field. Bobby gulped.

Cautiously, he parted the branches and peered through the bushes. There in the field was a huge creature. It had floppy ears, a red nose, and … yes … wiggly whiskers. It was a Sniffles! Bobby ran home as fast as his little legs would carry him.

"Bobby!" cried his mother. "We're so glad you're home. But whatever is the matter?"

When Bobby told his story to his family, Father Bunny set out to find the Sniffles. It turned out to be an old scarecrow!

Suddenly, Bobby felt a whole lot better. On the way home, his father explained what the sniffles really were.

"I've learned something very important tonight," announced Bobby with a smile. "It's not catching the sniffles you have to worry about, it's the sniffles catching you!"

The Teddy Bears' Picnic

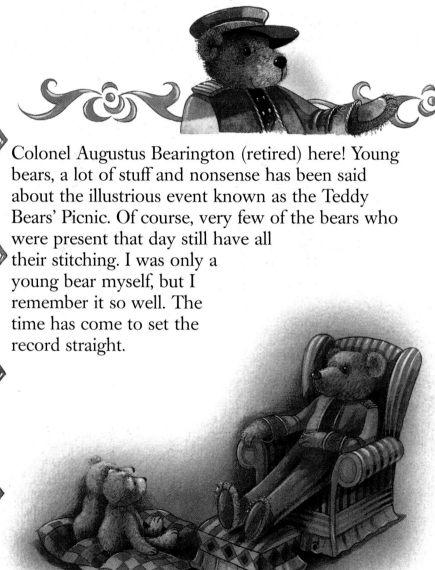

Colonel Augustus Bearington (retired) here! Young bears, a lot of stuff and nonsense has been said about the illustrious event known as the Teddy Bears' Picnic. Of course, very few of the bears who were present that day still have all their stitching. I was only a young bear myself, but I remember it so well. The time has come to set the record straight.

First of all you must remember that things were very different in those days.

Today, you young bears live in households that may have four or five bears. You have company and can rely on each other in times of trouble. In my young days, bears were less common. Only very lucky children lived with a bear of their own. A bear might stay in the same household for fifty years, passed down from father to son or kept on a shelf in the nursery.

179

Nurseries! That was another big difference. Children who shared their homes with bears usually spent most of their time in the nursery with a woman called a nanny. She looked after the children while their mother and father were busy, which was all the time except for half an hour in the evening.

Children had to be seen and not heard in those days, and nannies got very cross indeed if they didn't wash behind their ears. Today things are different. Very different indeed.

In those days, bears were not able to meet very often. The best chance was in the afternoon, when nannies took their charges to the park. Then children would play with friends from other big houses, nannies would chat and knit with other nannies, and bears, of course, could have a word with other bears. It was a part of the day that every bear looked forward to. Luckily, the nanny in the house where I lived liked nothing better than a long chat with her friends. No one paid any attention if a bear strolled off and kept up with his own social life.

I think it was Rufus who first
put the idea into our heads.
Rufus was a reddish-brown
bear from a rather well-to-
do home. The little girl he
lived with was a Lady. Yes,
a real Lady, whose mother
was a Duchess. I must say
that Rufus didn't let his
titled family go to his head.
He was a friendly, straight-
forward bear, who never put
on airs and graces.

One day, Rufus arrived
with interesting news. The
Duke and Duchess were giving a
party for some Very Important
People. There were whispers that the
Queen herself would be coming.

"You know, Gussie," said Rufus, "we bears should have a party of our own. We could invite all the Most Important Bears in town and have a day to remember."

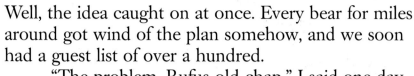

Well, the idea caught on at once. Every bear for miles around got wind of the plan somehow, and we soon had a guest list of over a hundred.

"The problem, Rufus old chap," I said one day, "is to find a place big enough for a party of this size. We can't run the risk of being discovered, you know."

Rufus didn't hesitate for a moment.

"We'll hold it right here," he said.

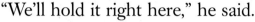

It was obvious! I was a muttonhead not to have thought of it myself. After that, there was no time to lose. I was in charge of arrangements, of course. It takes a military mind to organise an event on that scale. And, modesty aside, I must confess that I also came up with the date for the picnic. Army training came in useful for that, too.

Luckily, several young bears helped with the preparations. You'd be amazed what can be smuggled among a baby's blankets. There were cups, saucers, plates, and food, of course. And some cushions for the old bears. Damp grass is not good for their fur, you know.

At last the great day arrived. It was the day of the Queen's Jubilee. She had been on the throne for umpteen years, and her subjects lined the streets to cheer. Meanwhile, dozens of little bears padded along the back streets, heading for the picnic of a lifetime.

What an afternoon that was! I've never
seen so many bears having so much fun.

Ah, and that afternoon I met Rosabella.
But that's another story.

But someone did see us having the picnic, although we never knew who it was. Yes, there was a song. It was quite popular although the facts were wrong, of course. We were nowhere near the woods.

I still carry this worn photograph in my breast pocket after almost sixty years. Ah yes. It brings a lump to my throat just to look at all those fine faces. Bears were bears in those days.

The Bear Who Couldn't Stay Awake

My friends, the fire is burning low and the smallest bears have fallen asleep on our laps. Perhaps we should go off to bed now. What? One more story? Well, if you are sure.

This is the story of a very sleepy bear called Selina. Whenever she was wanted, Selina was always to be found dozing in a corner. Some bears were rather suspicious about Selina's sleeping. Somehow, when there was a treat in store, such as extra honey or a birthday party, Selina was always awake. When there was tidying to be done, or muddy paw prints to be removed, or honeypots to wash, Selina would be snoring quietly somewhere.

"If you ask me," grumbled the Oldest Bear of All, "that lazy little bear needs to be taught a lesson."

"Bears do need their sleep," explained her friend Marilyn anxiously. "Selina would be so upset if she knew what horrible things were being said about her. And she has slept right through suppertime. She wouldn't do that if she was really awake. She's always very hungry."

At that moment, Selina gave an extra loud snore.

The older bears shook their heads. "If she is pretending," they said, "she will wake up after we are asleep and have a little snack then. What we must do is stay awake tonight and watch carefully to see what happens."

So five bears volunteered not to go to bed. As it grew dark, they took up their positions and watched the sleeping Selina.

Very soon, the first little bear's nose began to twitch. He was trying to stop himself from yawning. Then his bright little eyes began to close. In just two minutes, he was fast asleep.

The second little bear struggled hard to stay awake. He patted his head with his paws to stop himself from drifting off to sleep. But his patting grew slower, and slower, and slower . . . until he too was dreaming a teddy bear dream.

The third bear was older than the first two. He was quite determined to stay awake. He decided to march up and down – quietly of course. *Pad, pad, pad*, he marched across the floor. *Pad, pad, pad*, back he came. *Pad, pad, pad . . . pad, pad, pad*. He looked as if he was wide awake. He sounded as if he was awake. But before long, that bear was sleep-walking! His eyes were closed, but his little legs were still moving. In his furry head, he dreamed of being a soldier on parade.

190

The fourth and fifth watching bears decided to keep each other awake. They talked in whispers late into the night. But there is something very soft and sleepy about whispering.

Although they tried hard to stay awake, soon the whispers became gentle snores.

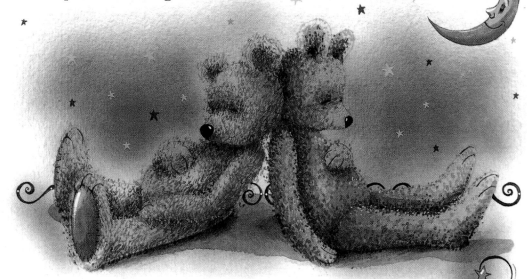

In the morning, the other bears crowded round them to see what had happened.

"Well . . . *ahem,*" said the first bear, "I certainly didn't see her wake up."
"Er . . . neither did I," agreed the second bear.

"I was on duty all night," said the third bear, "and I didn't hear a sound."

The fourth and fifth bears looked at each other, and scratched their furry heads. "I saw nothing unusual," said one, truthfully. "Did you, old pal?"

"Nothing at all," his friend replied firmly.

So the mystery of the sleeping bear never was solved. But Selina, who was sleeping happily in her usual place, gave an extra loud snore and the tiniest, sleepy, secret smile.

  Now it is time for little bears everywhere to go to sleep. Goodnight, little bears! Goodnight!